Married to the man she met at eighteen, **Susanne Hampton** is the mother of two adult daughters—one a musician and the other an artist. The family also extends to a slightly irritable Maltese shih-tzu, a neurotic poodle, three elderly ducks, and four hens that only very occasionally bother to lay eggs. Susanne loves everything romantic and pretty, so her home is brimming with romance novels, movies and shoes. With an interest in all things medical, her career has been in the dental field and the medical world in different roles, and now Susanne has taken that love into writing Mills & Boon® Medical Romance™.

Books by Susanne Hampton

Mills & Boon® Medical Romance™

Unlocking the Doctor's Heart
Back in Her Husband's Arms
Falling for Dr December
Midwife's Baby Bump

**Visit the author profile page at
millsandboon.co.uk for more titles**

Dedication

Thank you to Orianthi and Tina for being the most
wonderful daughters in the world. You are amazing
young women who appreciate your God-given gifts
and every day bring joy to those around you.
I am so proud of all that you have accomplished
and all that still lies ahead.

And once again thank you to Charlotte…
who always brings out the best in my writing…
and ensures I finish on time!

Praise for Susanne Hampton

'From the first turbulent beginning until the final
climactic ending, an entire range of emotions has been
used to write a story of two people travelling the rocky
road to love…an excellent story. I would recommend
this story to all romance readers.'
—*Contemporary Romance Reviews* on
Unlocking the Doctor's Heart

'I recommend this read for all fans of medical romance.
It's the perfect balance: spunky, emotional, heartfelt, a
very sweet and tender romance with a great message!'
—*Contemporary Romance Reviews* on
Unlocking the Doctor's Heart

PROLOGUE

JADE GRANT HUMMED along to the radio as she prepared dinner for one. The music was loud, just the way she liked it when there was no one around to complain about the volume. Occasionally she sang a few words, but remembering words to songs was not her strength, and neither, according to her sister, was her pitch, so mostly she stuck to humming.

Her bare feet danced a few steps on the way to the refrigerator. Her slim hips, dressed in faded denim shorts, swayed, and she managed a spontaneous spin in time to the music. While her voice left more than a little to be desired, dancing was something she was good at.

Opening the door on the beat, she bent down to peer inside then pulled some fresh broccoli and carrots from the crisper before she closed the door on the next beat and headed to the chopping board. Her new favourite song was blaring from the portable radio on the windowsill. A smile dressed her face and she felt good about life. It hadn't always been that way but finally she was in a happy place. Her career as a neonatal nurse was on track, she loved working at Los Angeles District Hospital and, although she wasn't dating anyone, there were more than a few residents paying her attention.

She wiped some tiny specks of broccoli from her cotton tank top before she glanced up at the clock on the wall and smiled. Her sister and brother-in-law would have arrived in Palm Springs and be in their happy place for the long weekend.

The hotel looked so luxurious online and the reviews were all good. Jade hoped that it would live up to the hype and Ruby and David would have a wonderful few days relaxing before their baby arrived. Ruby was just over six months pregnant and Jade wanted to give the pair a second honeymoon as she knew that once they were new parents their focus would be their baby. The way Ruby struggled with her pregnancy, and morning sickness that still hadn't abated, Jade wasn't sure how much of a honeymoon it would be, but it would at least be a getaway.

Ruby and David had taken Jade into their home after her ground-floor apartment had been flooded by a burst water main the previous month, and this was her small way to show appreciation. She planned on moving back in to her beach-side home as soon as repairs were completed but the insurance company was still arguing with the landlords so no date had been confirmed. Jade hadn't lost any personal belongings to the murky water, as she leased the apartment furnished, so it wasn't devastating, just inconvenient.

She finished chopping the vegetables and put them on to steam before she turned off the radio and went into the sitting room. While it was only temporary, it was still wonderful having a big house to herself for a few days, she thought as she sat down on the sofa. Her place in Santa Monica was quite small and the paper-thin walls allowed her to know far too much about her neighbours. Some mornings she found it difficult to look them in the eye in the car park. There were some things she just didn't want to know and some she found hard to forget. So Jade was enjoying everything about being in her big sister's house.

Collapsing back into the huge armchair, she threw her legs over the padded arms and reached for the remote control. It had been a long day on her feet at the hospital and she decided that after watching the six o'clock news and eating her dinner she would soak in the tub, read a book and turn in early.

Switching on the television, her mood abruptly fell as she saw the horrific footage of an eight-car pile-up on the Pacific Coast Highway that afternoon. Her stomach turned and heart fell with the sight of wreckage. Jade was carefree about a lot in life but not when it came to tragedies like the one playing out on the screen. It wasn't only the victims she thought about. Her prayers went out to the families whose lives would never be the same.

She and her sister had been one of those families. They had been left to pick up the pieces of their shattered lives when their mother and father had died in a road accident when Jade and Ruby had been in their late teens. It had been a turning point for both of them. Ruby, being the elder sister and feeling the need to take control, had changed almost overnight. She had become more cautious and wanted stability, while Jade had steered her life in the opposite direction. She had decided to make the most of every moment with the mantra that *life was short*.

The television showed the lights of the LAPD patrol cars flashing and ambulances parked randomly across the freeway near the mangled metal that trapped the victims against the cement pylons. Traffic was built up for miles in both directions. Every detail of the horror was being captured by the news helicopters hovering in the air above. Watching with a heavy heart, Jade assumed with dread that there would have been fatalities. With no dance in her step now, she returned to the stove and turned off the heat under the saucepan, just as she heard her telephone ringing inside her bag. There was no caller ID, she noticed, before she answered.

'Jade Grant?' the sombre female voice asked.

'Yes, speaking.'

'I'm Sergeant Meg Dunbar from the LAPD. I'm afraid there's been an accident on the Pacific Coast Highway. Your sister's been taken to Los Angeles District Hospital.'

Jade felt her head spin and her heart race with panic. 'No, it can't be. There's been a mistake. She's in Palm Springs with her husband.'

'I'm afraid she and her husband were involved in an accident on the PCH just over two hours ago. They finally cut your sister from the wreckage and she was transported here. She is still unconscious but I was able to get your details from her cell phone. Please come immediately, she's heading for the operating theatre. Her injuries are critical.'

'What about the baby?'

'Miss Grant, I'm sorry, I can't give you any further information about your sister's condition. I've told you everything I know. The doctors will tell you more when you get here.'

'And David, her husband, is he there with her?'

There was a moment's silence. 'I'm afraid, Miss Grant, your sister's husband didn't survive the accident.'

The phone crashed to the floor. Jade froze with her hands limp by her sides, her body trembling before she cried out loud and fell against the cold wall. The officer's words were ringing in her head, not unlike a siren. She could still see the footage of the accident on the screen and she realised David was lying there in the carnage. He had never reached Palm Springs. She couldn't speak or even find a logical thought at that moment. A numb feeling engulfed almost all of her body. Only her heart could feel anything, and that was unrelenting stabs of pain that threatened her breathing.

Eight years disappeared and suddenly Jade was the eighteen-year-old girl who had been told by the social worker that her parents had been killed. A heavily laden lorry had run a red light on the corner of Fairfax and Wilshire and they'd both died on impact. Jade remembered the distressed expression on the woman's face as she'd delivered the devastating news. She felt certain the policewoman on the other end of the phone had the same poignant expression. She didn't think that life could be so cruel and deliver her family the same overwhelming sadness twice. It was too much for one lifetime.

For a moment, she stared blankly at the wall, seeing nothing through the blur of her tears. But Jade couldn't fall to pieces the way she had all those years ago. Back then she'd had Ruby to tell her that everything would be all right and that they would always have each other. Reassuring Jade that she would always have someone to lean on through the hard times. Now Jade needed to hold herself together enough to stand strong beside her sister when she found out she had lost David. She had to be Ruby's pillar of strength this time.

Jade reached for her bag and keys as she brought herself back to reality, and to what remained of her shattered senses. She needed to get to the hospital. Ruby had just lost the love of her life and the father of her unborn child.

With tears running down her face, Jade ran for the door, and taking deep breaths she focused on the task of getting safely to the hospital. Their home was barely ten minutes from the Los Angeles District Hospital but it felt more like a lifetime away as she was stalled by the heavy evening traffic on Wilshire Boulevard. Every minute she sat there her heart was pounding in her chest and her stomach was churning with the reality of the crash that had claimed David's life.

Only a few hours before they had been in the kitchen together, talking about the wonderful few days ahead and thanking Jade for arranging their short holiday. David had planned on painting the nursery when they returned and Ruby was already filling the cupboards with baby clothes in preparation for the birth of their first child. They had been overjoyed when they'd been told it would be a little girl, just as they would have been overjoyed if they'd been told they were having a son. They had been so thrilled to be starting their family. She would be the first of four children, David had lovingly teased his wife as he'd patted her already rotund belly.

Finally Jade pulled into the hospital car park. Her tears had dried and she was steeling herself to be strong for Ruby as she stepped from the car. She had no idea that that was the same moment Ruby's heart stopped. Her sister had died on the operating table only minutes after having an emergency Caesarean to save the baby daughter she and David had already named Amber.

* * *

Jade wept openly and uncontrollably when she was told. Nothing the nurses or police could say would stop her tears. There was no amount of compassion or understanding that could stop her sobbing. She doubted the tears would ever cease and she knew her heart would never be whole again. This time she had no one to lean on.

'Will she live?' Jade asked, scared of the answer but still needing to know. She had kept vigil beside her tiny niece for every waking hour of the two days since her birth. She had dozed sitting upright.

'Jade,' the neonatologist said with an equal mix of warmth and authority tempering her voice, 'you know that Amber's having the very best care with the finest facilities.'

Jade sat in silence for a moment, gathering her thoughts before the shaky response slipped from her lips. 'I know, Dr Greaves, and I don't mean to be abrupt, but I don't want you to sugar-coat anything. I've been working here in the neonatal ICU for over two years now, so please just be honest with me about her prognosis.'

Jade watched the neonatologist as she cast her eyes down and her lips formed a hard line in her somewhat tired face. She knew that the paediatric specialist had been attending Amber all night and the toll of her dedication showed in the morning light. Her naturally thin features were further drawn. But Jade was as tired as the attending physician and that brought her close to becoming a victim of her emotions. She would rather appear forthright and detached at that moment than risk her arm reaching around her in a comforting way and reducing her to a useless, snivelling heap of guilt. Melissa Greaves was that type of doctor. Professional but also motherly. Jade made a space between them to make it difficult for Melissa to reach for her. She had to do this alone.

The doctor's hesitation in answering confirmed Jade's fears, and her stomach tensed with a hollow cramp. Her composed veneer of bravado was close to shattering.

Melissa turned to her with a look that signalled she was about to deliver the harsh reality. 'If complete honesty is to be the call then I have grave concerns for your niece. She's dropped below her very low birth weight of two pounds, only marginally, but every ounce is critical, as you know, Jade, with VLBW patients.' She paused for a moment as she slipped her pen inside her coat pocket.

'Amber's a little fighter but since you don't want me to lie to you, *if*, and that's a big *if*, she makes it through the day, I'd still only give her a fifty percent chance of survival. Her gestational age was twenty-nine weeks, so it was always going to be a struggle, but with the compromised maternal metabolic and cardiovascular factors brought about by the accident there are additional complications. With her mother trapped in the vehicle for almost two hours, there was decreased uterine blood flow and abnormal placental conditions prior to the emergency Caesarean, and she is a tiny baby, so Amber has a fight ahead if she is to survive.'

Anxiously, Jade turned to the tiny figure lying behind sterile glass walls. A sea of wires, all linked to monitors, supported her fragile life. Jade gently reached her hand through the porthole door of the incubator and gently stroked Amber's warm, wrinkled skin. She was like a tiny china doll. Despairingly, Jade looked at her tiny niece's beautiful face through the transparent head box that was supplying a constant stream of oxygen to make her breathing less difficult. All the while a drip was feeding nutrients through the sole of her swollen foot as the veins in her spindly arms had collapsed and had ceased being of any use for intravenous nourishment. The innocent child was fighting to survive, unaware that her parents' lives had been taken by the cruel hand of fate.

'You know, if there's a glimmer of light in all of this,' Melissa added, and crossed to Jade and gently placed a hand on her shoulder, 'Amber isn't suffering respiratory distress and her tiny lungs appear to be coping so she didn't need a ventilator. I am amazed and a little bewildered by this and it does give me reason to give you the fifty-fifty chance ratio. Without that, her survival would be much lower than fifty per cent. At birth, I placed her survival at less than twenty per cent.'

Jade took another deep breath. The odds were improving. However, the slight degree of optimism the doctor had imparted didn't bring her peace of mind. Jade wanted the one hundred per cent guarantee that she knew in reality no one could provide.

This environment was second nature to her, yet now being in neonatal ICU made her fearful. Every day, as a neonatal nurse, she cared for premature infants, yet seeing Amber needing the same level of intense assistance made her feel vulnerable. She had to pull herself together. Not for her sake but for Amber's. She had to be able to process what was happening and, if called upon, make the right and informed decisions regarding her niece's care.

'And you moved her from the open radiant warmer

last night?' Jade asked, appreciating and finding a level of comfort in the compassion she had tried to deflect.

'Yes. When you fell asleep for a few minutes in the early hours I decided that the increased stimulation from light and noise and the associated risk of decreased growth and weight gain was greater than the disadvantages of the incubator. She is just too tiny to lose any further body mass. The next twenty-four hours will be critical.'

'Then it looks like we're here together for another long day, Amber, but you will get through this,' Jade promised aloud to the sleeping infant, before adding silently, *And I will never leave your side. Never.* Trying unsuccessfully to quash her unshed tears, she turned away before Melissa witnessed her breakdown. Through a watery blur, she watched the shaky breathing of her niece's tiny body and felt so helpless it was overwhelming.

She had never felt so totally powerless before in her life. She wished she had saved every forgotten wish from each birthday cake over the past twenty-six years and could tie them together to wish for the one thing she wanted with all her heart. If only she could gently lift the spindly bundle from her tiny glass crib and softly whisper that everything would be all right. But she couldn't. There was no guarantee that everything would be all right. There were no promises of a future for this little girl clinging tenaciously to life. And if she did have a future it would be one without her mother and father.

The days passed slowly, but each hour that Amber lived gave Jade hope. The hospital granted her compassionate leave to focus on Amber. The baby's weight was stabilising and the doctors looked less worried, as did the neo-natal nurses, who were all friends as well as colleagues. None of them provided false hope but neither did they talk about the possibility that Amber might not survive.

Her heart ached for the baby she had been with for four days. A baby as wanted and loved as any child could be. She was the daughter that Ruby and David had dreamed of and planned for so many years. It made the bleakness of the prognosis so much harder to handle. She worried that not having her mother's love and natural bonding could add to the complications of Amber's early entry into the world. Although Jade wasn't her mother, she swore to herself she would be the next best thing and do everything in her power for the little girl at that moment and for the rest of her life. Amber had lost the mother she had never known but she would never lose Jade.

She would spend her life making it up to her niece for sending her parents on the holiday that had claimed their lives. And she would spend her life being the woman that Ruby and David would want raising their little girl.

But Jade was also struggling with her own grief. Grief the little girl knew nothing about. Over those first few days it was almost too much to bear. Not only was she close to crippled with worry about her niece, but she had also lost her sister. A sister she'd loved with all of her heart.

Ruby and Jade had been close all their lives and even more so after the loss of their parents. Ruby had been, in Jade's mind, the most wonderful sister in the world. She had been kind, and funny and nurturing. It was as if half of Jade was gone. Ripped from her life without warning. No chance to say goodbye. No opportunity to thank her sister for everything she had done. All the big sister advice she had given over the years. The advice that Jade had always appreciated but mostly ignored. The tears they had shed over boys who hadn't been worth it. The late-night calls to chat about nothing much but which had somehow lasted for hours.

It was all gone. She would never laugh with her sister again. She would never watch David look lovingly at his wife and hear them make plans and talk about their daughter's education. How Ruby would tell him that the little girl would be brighter than anyone else in the class because he was the father, and how he would say she would be without doubt the prettiest because she would look like her mother.

At times, Jade would tell them they sounded like a bad midday movie but their love for each other had been undeniable and real.

With that in mind, Jade held herself together. She owed it to Ruby and David to be there for their daughter and surround her with the love they would have lavished on her.

And then there was the added burden of guilt that sat heavily on her shoulders. No matter which way Jade looked at the situation, she felt responsible for Amber's early entry into this world. She had played the scene over and over in her mind since the accident. Why had she booked the holiday for them? If only she hadn't given them the present of a few days away in Palm Springs, they wouldn't have been a part of that terrible accident. And Amber would still be safely inside her mother with another ten weeks until her much-anticipated birth.

But instead, Jade was arranging the funeral of Amber's parents and staying strong for the tiny daughter they would never be able to love. She knew they both had a battle ahead but they would face it together. All they had now in the world was each other.

CHAPTER ONE

'WE ARE NOW commencing our descent into Adelaide.
Please ensure your tray table is secured and your seat
is in the upright position. We will be landing in fifteen
minutes and you will be disembarking at gate twenty-
three. Current time in Adelaide is eleven-thirty. Your
luggage will be available for collection on Carousel Five.
On behalf of the cabin crew, we hope you enjoyed your
flight and will fly again with us in the future.'

Jade wound up the cord of her headset before she
tucked it away after the flight attendant's announcement,
then, smiling, she looked over at her niece, still sleeping
soundly. She looked like a tiny angel. Her little round
face was resting in the pillow, her tight, strawberry-
blonde curls a little messy, her arm tightly holding her
rag doll and her bright blue eyes still hidden from the
world. It was the second leg of their travel. The fifteen-
hour-long haul from Los Angeles to Sydney had been
followed by a shorter flight to Adelaide.

The trip to Australia was not a journey that Jade had
wanted to make initially and one that she had been de-
laying, but she had known it was the right thing to do.
David's mother, Maureen, and stepfather, Arthur, had
wanted so much for their granddaughter to spend some

time in the town where their son, Amber's father, had grown up. So here they both were, about to touch down in a city that she remembered from David's conversations but a place she knew nothing about. Her stomach was churning nervously.

The last time she had seen Maureen and Arthur had been at the funeral almost three years before. It had been a time that Jade would never forget. Despite the overwhelming grief that no one had tried to mask, they'd shown great kindness in allowing David to be buried in Los Angeles with his wife. Jade knew that it would have been reasonable for them to want their son to be buried near them in his home town, but they had all known that David would want to be laid to rest with the woman he'd loved.

And so it was that they'd left their son for ever in a city eight thousand miles from them. It displayed a generosity of spirit, and Jade knew in her heart why David had been such a loving and considerate man. He had been his parents' son.

They had not visited Los Angeles again after the funeral, but Jade had accepted it would have been too sad to return to the place where their son had died. They had kept in contact with calls and emails and gifts for Amber's birthday and Christmas. Amber's birthdays were a bitter-sweet time for everyone as she had been born on the day her parents had both died. An unspoken agreement made them all try to celebrate the beautiful gift they had been given on that fateful day.

Jade felt an empty ache inside for what everyone had lost. Some nights she lay awake with her memories and overwhelming sadness. A trigger such as Amber's first step, first word, first anything reminded Jade of how

Ruby and David should be there to witness their daughter's milestones. And they weren't.

Amber never cried; she was too young to know what she was missing, and Jade was determined to devote her life to filling any gaps. Amber would never want for anything in her life. She would never be alone in the world.

As they walked across the air bridge, Jade spied David's mother and stepfather. Maureen was beaming with excitement, her smile so wide that Jade could see it before she entered the arrival lounge. Arthur's expression was more stoic, almost stern, but she knew he was a good man and a generous one. Maureen was dressed in a pastel floral summer dress and wore flat gold sandals, her blonde hair cut in a short, modern style. Arthur wore long beige trousers with a navy and cream checked shirt, his hair silver grey. They were a stylishly conservative couple, sharing David's dress sense, Jade thought.

Holding Amber's tiny hand in hers, Jade walked up the carpeted incline to where the couple were waiting. Still a little drowsy, Amber was struggling to hold on to her ragdoll, and the soft legs dragged behind them into the terminal.

'Hello, Maureen,' Jade said, and kissed the woman's cheek lightly. Then she greeted Arthur with a kiss to his sun-wrinkled cheek. Jade wondered if it was tennis or golf that had weathered his happy face. Now retired, he had spent his working life as a surgeon so she knew it wasn't from toiling in the midday sun.

'Amber, sweetheart, this is Grandma and Grandpa.'

'Hello, Amber, I hope you both had a good trip,' Maureen said, directing her comment to Jade as she wrapped her arms around Amber and kissed her ruddy, warm cheek.

'Hello,' came Amber's shy, almost muttered reply. Jade noticed her niece flinch and wriggle before she leant back, wanting to be in her arms. Understanding the little girl's reticence at being embraced by a woman she didn't know, Jade gently reached for her.

'She's a bit tired,' she said apologetically, and she lifted the child, who was now looking quite worried, almost teary, into her arms 'It was a long flight, but I certainly couldn't complain. It was very generous of you to fly us here first class.'

'Nonsense, we wouldn't have it any other way,' Maureen announced, still stroking the little girl's arm, and to Jade's relief not offended by the child's reaction. 'Nothing is too good for either of you. You are family and our home is your home for as long as you can stay. I'm hoping you love Adelaide so much you won't ever leave. We have such a big house all to ourselves.'

Smiling, Arthur rolled his eyes at the complete lack of subtlety in his wife's announcement, took hold of Jade's carry-on luggage, and together, the four of them made their way to collect the checked-in luggage.

Jade smiled at the warmth and genuine sentiment in Maureen's words. But it would never happen. Their lives were in Los Angeles and they were in Adelaide for one month. It was all the leave she could take from Cedars Sinai, where she still worked but now part time. Jade had thought about leaving when Amber had been discharged to her care. She had wondered how she would pull into the car park of the hospital where her sister had passed away. But over time it gave her comfort to know she was where Ruby had spent her last moments of life. And where Amber had taken her first breath.

But now they were in Adelaide and, despite being a

little weary, Jade was happy she had made the trip. Maureen and Arthur had lost their son and they deserved to spend time with their granddaughter. It would be Amber's third birthday while they were together and the third anniversary of Ruby and David's death. They could both console each other and celebrate together.

As they all headed down the escalators, Arthur insisted on collecting their bags from the luggage carousel so Jade and Amber could enjoy the sun outside.

'Go on, head outside and stretch your legs,' he told Jade.

'Amber's case is bright pink with yellow polka dots,' Jade replied as she scooped up the rag doll, now a little grubby from being dragged through the airport, and put it in her oversized handbag. 'Mine's a little less embarrassing for you. It's a silver hard-shell suitcase with a red luggage tag.'

Arthur smiled, handed Maureen Jade's carry-on and headed over to wait with the other passengers and families for the luggage to arrive.

Slipping on her sunglasses, Jade stepped out under the brilliant blue sky with Amber stuck by her side like a magnet. The sun felt good on her face. Perhaps a break like this was just what they both needed.

'We can't tell you how excited we both are to have you and Amber here, Jade.'

Jade turned and smiled at Amber's grandmother. The joy in Maureen's face made the long flight worthwhile to Jade. 'We're very happy to be here.'

It wasn't long before Arthur reappeared with the two large suitcases and they were on their way to the high-rise airport car park.

'Uncle Mitchell might be there when we get home,'

Maureen said to Amber, who in turn showed little reaction to the words of the nice older lady she didn't know.

Jade was momentarily confused. *Uncle Mitchell?* Then quickly the fog of the long flight lifted and she remembered David's brother. Although last she'd heard he was still living in some remote part of the world. He was the older but immature brother who never settled down but instead travelled widely and lived his life as one great big adventure. Like a nomad who pitched a tent wherever the mood took him.

'Isn't Mitchell living overseas?'

Maureen ran her fingers gently through Amber's mess of curls that Jade realised badly needed a brush. This time Amber didn't flinch, and Jade surmised that her niece had worked out that Maureen posed no threat. Jade hoped the two would grow close quite quickly, as their time together would be limited and precious.

'No, Mitchell's here in Adelaide at the moment. He's been in Africa for over four years but he came home a few months ago. Not long after he heard you were planning on visiting. Quite a coincidence really.' She raised her gaze to meet Jade's and with a knowing look added, 'I think he knew we needed him. Although he'll never admit it. He's quite the independent type but I think he was worried about all of us. Not sure how long he'll stay, though, as he's not one to lay down any roots. But still, he's here and he has the opportunity to meet you and celebrate his niece's birthday and that is all that matters.'

Jade didn't give it much thought. Her focus was to repay Arthur and Maureen for their kindness in the only way she could—by allowing them to spend time with Amber. Uncle Mitchell could waltz in and out as he pleased, which, from everything she had heard, was his style. No fixed address for any extended period appeared to be his way of life and it didn't look as if it had changed.

Mitchell's devil-may-care way of life was not her concern. She had met men like him before and had dated a few of them but that was in her past. And she had no intention of treading in that territory again. When it came to men Jade was numb. She didn't hate men, but she certainly didn't need a man in her life any more. Her priorities had changed the night of the accident. She didn't have time to think about men or relationships. They no longer factored into her life.

Now her focus was Amber, her work at the hospital and building a happy, secure life for the two of them. Men were a distraction and she didn't have room in her life for any distractions. She owed her sister and David her undivided attention to their daughter. She had promised them both that in her prayers the night Amber had been born.

'So how is little Amber doing?' Arthur asked matter-of-factly, as he inserted his validated parking ticket into the machine and waited for the arm to rise and release them. 'I know she's had a number of medical issues but she's a far cry from the infant we saw in ICU. She looks the picture of health now.' As he spoke, the automated arm lifted, and they left the car park and headed in the direction of the main road that would lead to their beachside residence.

Jade looked down at Amber, who was still drowsy and now sucking her thumb. The last time she'd seen Maureen and David had been at the funeral and when they'd visited Amber in hospital. She had been less than a week old and a little over two pounds by then. The little girl had been through so much over the years and there were still potential medical hurdles ahead, but Jade tried not to dwell on them. She was also aware that Arthur was a retired orthopaedic surgeon so he had the understanding and ability to process the medical details.

'As I said in my emails, Amber was diagnosed with dysplasia in her right kidney.'

'What's kidney dysplasia and is it serious?' Maureen interrupted.

'It means, darling,' Arthur began to explain as he watched the lights change at the intersection, 'that one of little Amber's kidneys didn't develop properly before she was born and she has fluid-filled sacs instead of healthy tissue in one kidney, but the other one is perfectly fine and doing the work of both.'

'Can that go on indefinitely or will the good kidney be overworked?' Maureen's question was directed at both Jade and Arthur.

Arthur looked over at his wife with a knowing expression. She had no medical knowledge but she was an intelligent and inquisitive woman and they were two of the many reasons he had married her. He knew she would have excelled in any field she had chosen so he did not need to over-simplify his medical terminology around her.

'A baby or, in Amber's case, a young child with one working kidney can grow normally without too many health problems. Babies with kidney dysplasia affecting both kidneys generally do not survive pregnancy, and those who do survive need dialysis and a kidney transplant very early in life.'

'How dreadful for the child and the parents.'

Jade stroked Amber's forehead gently and watched

her precious niece holding on tightly to the favourite rag doll she had pulled from Jade's bag.

'We are fortunate, but Amber is still being closely monitored back in LA,' Jade added.

'How did it happen?' Maureen asked as they left the highway.

'Kidney dysplasia can have genetic causes,' Jade replied, imparting the information as if she were back at the hospital, rather than talking about the little girl dozing by her side. It was easier that way. 'It appears to be a dominant trait, which means one parent may pass the trait to a child. Normally, when this is discovered, the child's parents undergo an ultrasound to confirm if either have the condition but this wasn't possible for Amber so we will never know if it was Ruby or David. And really it's a moot point,' she said as the car headed over a small bridge. Jade could see the shimmering ocean ahead and she looked forward to spending a few weeks by the beach, not overthinking what might lie ahead. She knew what she might face in the future with Amber's condition and, as always, it was upsetting just to think about it.

'But the important thing is our granddaughter is healthy and that makes me happy.'

'Amber is healthy now,' Jade confirmed, then paused for a moment to gather her thoughts and not become emotional. She was tired from the flight and she tried not the think about the potentially life-threatening condition that Amber could face if her functioning kidney were to fail. 'She's monitored closely and I suppose that's why it took so long for us to get here. I wanted to make sure she was well enough to fly and not compromise or exacerbate her condition.'

'So she got the all-clear to be here from her paediatric nephrologist in LA?' Arthur asked as he indicated and turned into their street.

'Yes, Dr Mulligan said it would be fine but he gave me the details for the renal unit at the Eastern Memorial Hospital should there be any issues.'

'That's my old stomping ground. I only retired last year,' Arthur responded with a touch of melancholy colouring his voice.

'Yes, I remember that from one of your emails, so it's comforting that you know the hospital well,' she returned. 'But let's hope we won't need to visit there as she had an examination with Dr Mulligan only two days before we left and he said that she is progressing well and may travel through life with no other issues. That's the best-case scenario, but if we aren't that fortunate, I hope treatment is many years away and she is old enough to understand it. Although she will need genetic counselling when, and if, she wants children of her own one day.'

'Goodness, children of her own. That's such a very long time away. Let's not rush the poor child.' Maureen turned around and once again looked proudly at her only grandchild. Her happiness was contagious and lifted Jade's spirits again.

'So there's no need to think she'll be anything other than fine and she can look forward to spending four lovely weeks with us,' Arthur retorted, purposely lifting the tone of his voice.

'And her Uncle Mitchell,' Maureen added, happiness evident in her voice.

Uncle Mitchell. Jade was taken aback yet again at hearing his name. Although she was far from curious about the elusive Mitchell, apparently she was finally going to meet him and so was Amber. The seemingly irresponsible brother with wanderlust. Ruby and David had eloped so there had never been a wedding to allow the families to meet. Although it wouldn't have been a huge gathering as there had not been much of a family on Ruby's side. There had only been Jade and Ruby.

Jade suspected that was why David had suggested eloping. The idea of David's family filling one side of the church and their side empty but for their friends would have made the day bitter-sweet and that was why she assumed he'd arranged an impromptu sunset wedding in Maui. He had been a considerate and devoted man. And from what she had heard completely at odds with his brother.

Mitchell hadn't travelled over for the funeral but Jade had been dealing with her own insurmountable sadness so she hadn't been too aware of anyone else and their presence or lack thereof then. It had been a sad time that she wanted to both forget and remember. Remember because it had been her last connection to the sister she'd loved completely, and forget because she hadn't thought she would survive the sense of loss that had threatened her sanity during those weeks and months that had followed the accident.

But apart from his lack of interest in his brother's funeral, Jade knew little about Mitchell. Over the years postcards and photographs from far-away places had arrived, somewhat battered, and the very occasional email when Mitchell had been somewhere with an internet connection. Jade had seen them pinned to the corkboard in her sister's kitchen when she'd visited. It had been difficult to see what he looked like behind the wraparound sunglasses he'd worn in all the shots. But scruffy and rough around the edges was the lasting impression. His hair was long and wild, almost in dreadlocks, and so, too, was his beard. David, on the other hand, had been clean cut and well mannered. And Mitchell appeared to have a new girlfriend in each photo.

For some reason, David's face would light up when he'd looked at the photographs and the reverence he'd felt for his brother had been clear. He would say proudly that Mitchell was the most selfless person in the world and the best brother, but neither Ruby nor Jade had been able to see any evidence of it.

The brothers had had a bond that had stretched across the continents and oceans that had separated them, and Ruby would often say that she never understood what was so admirable about his carefree, and from the content of the photographs, playboy lifestyle. The bungee jumping, abseiling and mountain climbing all pointed to an adrenalin-driven way of life. He was a nomad and spent a great deal of time in countries on the African continent. Nothing like the life that David had chosen. Ruby and David had been so perfectly suited and Jade had been happy for her sister.

Jade was not like her sister, though. She had never found the man perfectly suited to her. Although she wasn't actively searching, either. Her mantra drove her to live a full life and not rush to settle down. She had dated a few men, including an up-and-coming musician who had left town to make it on the East Coast, then a pro-football player while she'd been at college and a bull rider during her first nursing placement. Jade had liked the idea that she'd been with a man involved in what was called the most dangerous eight seconds in sport but the fascination had quickly faded and Jade had lost interest, just like she had with the others. There had been something missing. They'd had fun times but there had been no real connection. She hadn't been looking for *the one* but even if she had been she hadn't found him.

Ruby had not liked any of Jade's boyfriends. She'd thought her taste had been deteriorating, not improving, and hadn't hidden her aversion to what had appeared to be Jade's less-than-desirable type. She'd worried that the way her sister had dressed might have had something to do with the men she'd attracted and she oftentimes would suggest a more demure style, like her own, but Jade had loved her shorts and T-shirts. Ruby had complained that the men Jade had liked had been too wild and a man who couldn't be tamed would never be for keeps. Jade hadn't been looking for for ever, like her sister; she'd been happy to just enjoy a life without ties. She'd lived for the moment. A serious relationship had held little or no appeal.

She'd just been too busy enjoying life and having fun because *life was short*.

Looking back now, Jade reluctantly admitted to herself that Mitchell's ongoing carefree life was not too far from her former life. Her life before she'd become Amber's guardian. A life that she had almost forgotten. She had been skydiving more than once and had loved it. The rush that had engulfed her mind and her body as she'd been freefalling towards the ground just before the chute had opened had been thrilling. Her heart had raced, and she'd felt alive and exhilarated, but now her feet would be firmly placed on the ground. Now she wouldn't even contemplate a roller-coaster ride at Six Flags, her once favourite theme park and the destination of her former regular weekend trek with friends.

Now there was nothing in the world more important than taking care of her niece and making sure they were both safe at all times. The old free spirited Jade Grant was now very tame and very conservative in every possible way. Her once long blonde hair was now a short pixie cut, her clothes were more in keeping with someone at least ten years older and her make-up non-existent save for some tinted sunscreen and lip gloss. She was doing her best in every way to be exactly the person Amber needed and that Ruby and David would have wanted to be her daughter's guardian. The old Jade had been packed away. She wanted Amber to feel safe and the best way she knew how to do that was to be more like Ruby. Sensible was now her middle name.

'Here we are,' Arthur announced as he pulled the SUV into the driveway of the luxurious three-storey home. The architecture was modern, with a large glass balcony on both upper floors overlooking the beach.

Jade lowered her glasses. The home was palatial and the view as she stepped out of the car and looked around was spectacular.

'It's beautiful. What part of Adelaide is this?'

'Glenelg… North Glenelg, to be exact,' Arthur said with pride as he lifted the cases from the back of the vehicle. 'Just love it here, like an all-year-round holiday but still so close to the city. And you can go surfing if you'd like. Mitchell's renting a condo just down the road, walking distance actually, but it has on-road parking, with no storage space so he leaves his surfboard in our garage. I'm sure he wouldn't mind if you borrowed it. I remember David telling us you were quite a surfer girl.'

Jade froze. *Surfer girl?* That had been a lifetime ago. And it was a pastime that she would never contemplate again. Now that love of riding a wave was tainted by the reality that she could easily be knocked unconscious by her own board and drown at the bottom of the ocean. Surfing was right up there with the all the other activities from her past. Something she'd once done during summer break with her friends at Malibu but something that she would never consider now. With every day she found a greater understanding of how Ruby had seen life. And how that was needed, for Amber's well-being.

'I'm not a surfer any more, or even much of a swimmer, to be honest, but I'm sure Amber will love building sandcastles.'

'I'm sure she will. And the shops are close by, too,' Maureen added, hoping to bond with Jade over a shared love of shopping. Struggling to bring up two sons on her own, before she'd met Arthur much later in life, hadn't allowed her to share too much but now with Jade and Amber she thought they could enjoy some time together and buy lots of pretty things for her granddaughter.

Jade walked around to open the door and reach in for Amber.

'May I?' Maureen asked as she moved towards the car.

Jade wasn't sure how Amber would react but she politely stepped back and was pleasantly surprised when the little girl allowed her grandmother to lift her from the car. Jade stayed close at hand so Amber would stay relaxed. A smile overtook Maureen's pretty face and she carried Amber, and the grubby rag doll, up the steps to the front door.

'Perhaps you and your doll might like a nice bubble bath before lunch,' Maureen said softly, and waited for Arthur to unlock the door to the home that they would all share for the next four weeks.

Jade smiled as she entered the second guest bathroom half an hour later. She knelt down next to Maureen and watched her fuss over Amber as she played in the large white porcelain tub of warm bubbles. Jade had enjoyed a relaxing shower in another marble-tiled bathroom before she'd towel-dried her short hair and changed into an ankle-length cotton sundress. Long showers were a rarity as she didn't like to leave Amber alone for too long, but safe in the knowledge that Maureen had the little girl, and that she seemed content to spend time with her grandmother, Jade had taken her time and let the hot water and steam massage her tired body.

It had been almost three years of being the sole provider and now she knew that Amber was happy spending time with her grandparents Jade was looking forward to a few luxuries, like the occasional long, hot shower, over the next few weeks. But she still wouldn't be too far away.

She had heard laughter as she had approached the bathroom. Amber had a bright pink-and-white floral bath cap perched on her head but more than a few curls had slipped out and were now decorated with bubbles. The bathtub was filled with colourful plastic bath toys that Jade suspected had been purchased just for Amber. There were no other grandchildren and the toys looked far too new to have once belonged to David or Mitchell.

The next four weeks no doubt would be a time for spoiling Amber, and Jade was not about to tell Arthur or Maureen otherwise. Amber had been through so much and she deserved every bit of happiness and love that could be given to her. And equally Arthur and Maureen had suffered a terrible loss and she was happy that they could finally spend time with their only link to their son, their gorgeous granddaughter.

'What about we all head over to the beach to build a sandcastle after you're all clean?'

'Well, that makes no sense at all!' came a deep male voice from behind them.

Jade jumped a little with surprise. It wasn't Arthur's voice and she had not heard any steps, but looking around she immediately knew why. She saw two very tanned bare feet that would have made no noise on the tile corridor leading to the bathroom. Slowly, her gaze rose to equally tanned legs and then low-slung board shorts. When her eyes met the perfectly sculpted abs and chest, she felt her heart race a little underneath her thin cotton dress. It was a feeling she had not experienced in a very long time.

It was a feeling she didn't want or need. And it rattled her usual calm demeanour.

'You wash a child and then take her to roll in the sand. She'll look like a piece of crumbed chicken.'

'Mitchell, don't be awful,' Maureen scolded him light-heartedly without turning around. Her attention didn't waver from her granddaughter in the water. 'Amber has flown for almost twenty hours so she needed to clean up. I'll dry her before we head to the sand and she is much too beautiful to ever look like crumbed poultry.'

Jade started to climb to her feet as the banter continued. Her long dress was caught around her knees and ankles and made it difficult to get up quickly.

'I thought I heard you up here,' Arthur cut in, and patted Mitchell on the shoulder. 'You're in time to meet Jade, Amber's aunt…'

'Oh, I know who Jade is,' Mitchell replied, and put out a hand to help Jade up. 'Pleased to finally meet you.'

Jade felt obliged to accept his hand, but she was pleasantly surprised that it wasn't grubby and in keeping with his jungle appearance in the photos. It was clean and warm and strong. Immediately, she almost wished she had refused. Slowly, she stood to her feet and came face to face with the man she had heard so much about—the wanderer who never stayed anywhere long, the brother whom David had loved and admired, and the man who she now knew enjoyed teasing his mother.

And the man who immediately took her breath away.

He was not scruffy, not even close. His long blond hair, once wild and dirty, was very short and well groomed, his long beard replaced by a fine covering of dark stubble and his eyes, always hidden behind sunglasses in the photos, were the brightest shade of blue. As clear and brilliant as the sky she had seen when she'd arrived a few hours ago.

It couldn't be the same man. This man was gorgeous. And as he gently pulled her to him to softly kiss her cheek, she smelt the fresh overtones of his cologne. Her senses were suddenly overloaded.

'Aunty Jade, catch!'

Jade turned her attention back to her niece to see a soapy plastic duck heading towards her. Instinctively, she moved to catch the airborne object but caught her sandal on the bathmat, losing her footing. She tried to steady herself but was swaying precariously. Suddenly, Mitchell's firm hands reached out and caught her. She fell into his arms and his mouth hovered only inches from hers. His touch was warm on her bare shoulders and his strength kept her upright until she gathered her composure and could do it for herself. Her stomach began to churn nervously. Her reaction and feelings surprised her. No man had affected her that quickly for a very long time. Then she mentally corrected herself. No man had *ever* affected her that quickly.

'Are you all right?' His voice matched his appearance. It was as deep as the tan of his skin and very masculine.

She stepped back and smoothed down her dress. Words had completely escaped her and his nearness made her conscious of his sensuality. Astoundingly, he had managed to remind her of her own. It was ridiculous, she knew it. She had no interest in men. Any men. They were off limits to her. She had signed a deal with herself to forget dating, to forget men in general until Amber was married or at least enrolled in college. And by that time she surmised she would probably have no appeal for them, or them for her. It hadn't been a hard deal to keep. The men she had dated previously, *her type*, no longer appealed. In fact, no man had been appealing since the accident. But somehow Mitchell's touch had left her dizzy.

His expression was serious and his concern seemed genuine but she knew his type, a very handsome drifter with no ties. What she didn't know was why she was reacting this way. There was something about the man, other than his looks, that was attracting her to him. Then she realised that looking into his eyes was like looking into Amber's. The stunning blue eyes staring back at her were the same colour as those of the little girl she had kissed goodnight for almost three years. He was a part of the little girl as much as she was. They both shared a special bond with their beautiful niece.

But looks alone was where his bond ended. The bond of family was one he had chosen not to act on. He had never tried to see Amber. Mitchell had apparently been too busy enjoying life to bother checking in on his niece. He'd left that role to Jade and although she was more than happy to be the sole caregiver, the occasional call might have been nice. It might have shown that he actually had a heart and cared.

Mitchell hadn't displayed any interest in the little girl up to now so she wasn't about to just let him step into Amber's life without any scrutiny. And without a damned good explanation.

He had returned home to spend time with his parents for reasons known only to him and at a strangely coincidental time, but Jade supposed the shine would wear off the situation and he would be riding back into the sunset very soon. His type was nothing new to her.

'I'm fine,' she finally mouthed, still confused by the way he was affecting her, given the situation. Bringing her niece to Australia was not about to change the way she looked at men, or didn't look, as the case had been.

The idea that she could in any way be attracted to Amber's uncle was ludicrous. She snapped her wandering thoughts back to reality. She was beyond angry with him for not investing some time in his niece over the past three years, although she wasn't about to take him to task over it on meeting him. Maureen and Arthur deserved better than that. They were gracious and generous to a fault and she would not show any animosity to their son in front of them. And she also didn't want Amber to feel anything but love when she thought of her family so she wouldn't let on how she really felt about Mitchell when anyone else was around. That was between the two of them.

Jade was aware that Amber might ask questions about Mitchell as she grew up, but she had already planned on being diplomatic about the absent uncle purely out of respect for David. She owed nothing to Mitchell so it was not out of respect for him.

Jade planned on asking the hard questions when they were alone. She deserved to know why he had never bothered to reach out and get to know the little girl who was a living bond to the brother who had adored him. Jade did not understand how he could move on with his life and not want the child to be a part of it. It made no sense at all to her.

Neither had her feelings when he'd touched her. Suddenly, nothing made sense. How could she be attracted to a man she resented? It was ridiculous.

'Are you sure you're okay?' Mitchell gave her a wary look as he studied her. She was pretty, very pretty, he thought, but she appeared quite uptight. Almost like a governess. Her dress was plain, not unlike something a farmer's wife or librarian might have in their closet. It was safe, almost virginal. Then the word came to him. *Prim.* Jade's appearance was the epitome of primness. Proper and nice and completely disguising any sign of her womanly curves. The hem of her sundress was just above her ankles so even her legs were almost hidden from view. Her arms were bare but he suspected she would have a cardigan or shawl close by. Her hair was practical and he saw there was no sign of make-up, although she truly did not need it anyway. She was naturally pretty.

Yet this woman before him did not match the one described by David as Ruby's wild-child sister. The one who lived life like one long party. Mitchell had arrived at his parents' home expecting a fun-loving Daisy Duke and was sadly disappointed. There was no reality he knew in which wild-child and Jade would sit comfortably side by side. They were poles apart—in fact, Mitchell thought there was close to a universe dividing them. He had imagined from his brother's reports that they would have much in common and would enjoy spending time together while she was in town. But as he had no interest in spending time at the local library, it wasn't going to happen. Life was short and he wasn't about to waste any of it.

It was a not a coincidence that he had returned while Jade and Amber were in town. He had wanted to meet her and extend his condolences. Something he hadn't been able to do after the accident. He had been working in a remote village with Doctors Without Borders and he hadn't managed to secure passage home in time for the funeral. There had been no internet or phone coverage and he'd only found out about the accident the day before the service. After that he'd seen no point in going. He hadn't wanted to fly to the US and have expectations and responsibility put upon him the moment he landed. He was not father material and suspected that, however wild, Jade would be a better guardian for Amber. Better by far.

Coming to Australia meant he could meet Jade and Amber and then disappear again back to his own life and leave them to theirs. He'd wanted to meet his niece more than anything and it had torn at him not to have done so before, but he'd been afraid about the damage he might cause by raising expectations he couldn't meet. He hadn't wanted to step into their lives when he had no intention of staying.

But this visit was different. It was a holiday and that in his mind equated to no residual scars for any of them. It was neutral territory for the meeting. Jade and Amber would have Maureen and Arthur to depend on in the future if the need arose. It was a better option all round.

He had, however, imagined he might enjoy his time with Jade. With everyone in holiday mode it might be fun, but looking at her now he felt sure that the word *fun* was not in her dictionary. He wondered how his older brother's idea of wild could be that different from his own.

Or had Jade changed?

Something just didn't add up.

'I'm absolutely fine,' she responded politely, and turned away from what she found to be a scrutinising gaze from an absurdly handsome man whom she wanted to scold for his apathy where his niece was concerned.

'Are you ready to build some sandcastles?' Jade asked Amber to steer her mind and mouth from telling him what she was really thinking.

'Yeth, pleath,' came the lisped reply.

Maureen laughed and reached into the warm water and pulled the bathplug free. 'Grandma will lift you out then, sweetheart,' Maureen began as she pulled the little girl from her watery surroundings and wrapped her in the fluffy white towel.

'Amber, this is your uncle Mitchell.'

Mitchell dropped to his knees and put out his hand. Amber met it with a handshake.

'Very pleased to meet you, Amber,' Mitchell said softly. Then, looking from side to side, he added, 'If you want some fun away from the fuddy-duddies you call me and we'll go pony riding or maybe up to the Monarto Zoo, where they have lions and tigers and bears... Oh, my...'

Amber giggled at him. *The Wizard of Oz* was one of her favourite movies.

'I think that Amber will be just fine building sandcastles,' Jade cut in firmly with an expression of horror. *Lions and horseback riding?* Was he completely mad? Not a word or sight of the man in almost three years and now he wanted to whisk his niece off on a wildlife adventure and call it a fun day out. Hell would freeze over before she would let him take Amber anywhere.

'Then I guess I'll leave you ladies to it,' Mitchell said, climbing back to his feet and stepping back. He tried to mask his confusion and disappointment. He had been looking forward to spending time with the fun-loving Jade he had heard about but this very tame version was definitely giving him the cold shoulder. He got the message loud and clear. They had nothing in common, except their fondness of the little girl now walking like an Egyptian mummy in her oversized towel towards the door.

'There's a great breeze up now so I'm going to spend the afternoon windsurfing.' With that, he disappeared from the doorway.

'Don't forget the sunblock.' His mother's words echoed down the hallway after him.

'I'm thirty-six years of age and I've spent four years

in Africa and two in Saudi Arabia so I think I'll be just fine.' He shook his head and waved goodbye but didn't turn around.

Jade watched his mother's lips curve into a smile. There was clearly something in Mitchell that made his mother happy, but Jade wasn't buying it. To her, he was selfish and self-serving. Extremely handsome, she conceded, but that was not the point, she reminded herself. He was everything she didn't want or need to influence Amber's choices in life.

'Really, Maureen, do you want to scare your son away again?' Arthur asked with a grin as he scratched his shaking head. 'He's an adult, so just do your helicopter mothering with little Amber... And be careful, Jade, she'll have her sights on doing the same to you if you let her.'

Jade knew she had to mask the animosity she felt for Mitchell. She would be happy if he windsurfed for the entire four weeks and left them alone. Or, better yet, a huge gust took him safely back to Africa.

She was unnerved by the man. She didn't like the feeling at all. Although she didn't like simmering anger either, it was preferable to what he was stirring inside her.

Her pulse had slowed after he'd left and that was how it needed to stay, she thought as she followed Amber and Maureen back to the guest room. It was a pretty room, decorated in soft peach hues with two double beds and a view of the beach. The balcony doors were closed, and Jade intended on keeping them that way, even though she knew the high glass-and-chrome balustrade would more than protect Amber. *Better safe than sorry* was her new mantra. *Life is short* had been replaced the day she had held Amber in her arms for the first time.

'There's another guest room but I thought Amber would want you to sleep in the same room as it's a strange house to her.'

'She would, thank you.'

'I bought a few bits and pieces for Amber to wear here and then take back home to America with you,' Maureen announced, and slid open one of the built-in wardrobe doors to reveal clothing fit for a little princess or three. 'I wasn't sure what Amber's favourite colour was—'

'So she bought them in every colour,' Arthur cut in, rolling his eyes before he walked away and left the women to themselves.

'It's too much. It will never fit in her suitcase,' Jade said softly, not wanting to offend Maureen but also aware that Amber shouldn't become accustomed to a lavish lifestyle as she would not be able to keep it up when they returned to Los Angeles.

Amber and Jade were living in the home that David and Ruby had bought. Although it was sad at times, Jade thought that it was important for Amber to grow up surrounded by her parents' belongings. The house had been left to Jade and Mitchell in the will but Mitchell had sent a message through his lawyer that he wanted his share given to Amber. She had sent a letter back to him through the lawyer, showing her gratitude at his generosity, but she'd never received a reply. She didn't know if he hadn't received her thanks or if he'd just chosen to ignore them.

Either way, Jade had left it alone. Whatever his reasons, he had given Amber his share of the property and his actions did allow them to own a house. It was a lovely home in Hancock Park, not too far from the hospital. Her neighbours were an older couple who had never been blessed with children and they were very happy to babysit Amber when Jade was working. They'd told her it was better that she got out of the house and they loved the time they spent with the little girl. She was like the grandchild they'd never had.

But working only part time didn't allow for too many luxuries. Jade had invested the insurance money that David and Ruby had left behind to ensure that Amber had her college education well covered.

'Nonsense,' Maureen replied. 'I will have them shipped back to LA for you. Now, what about shorts and a pretty top for the beach?'

'That would be lovely,' Jade responded, accepting that Maureen had every right to spoil Amber and it would save her buying clothes for at least two years, judging by the number of outfits decorating the brightly coloured hangers. 'Her favourite colour this week is yellow.'

'Yeth, yellow!' Amber said, jumping up and down and losing her towel, which fell to the floor.

Maureen looked up at Jade with a knowing smile. 'Then yellow it is, Missy Amber,' she said, giving the little girl a yellow bikini before she pulled a pair of yellow shorts with daisies embroidered on the pockets and a yellow-and-pink-striped top with pretty capped sleeves.

Jade walked over to the long line of glass doors as Maureen happily helped the little girl into her new outfit. The breeze had picked up, sending white-tipped waves gently rolling into the shore. The huge expanse of sand was dotted with large colourful beach umbrellas. The Australian coastline was even more stunning than she had imagined.

Suddenly, something caught her eye, and she saw a figure crossing the road below. She leant forward against the glass and recognised Mitchell. He was carrying his windsurfing board to the steps that led to the beach. His broad shoulders were tanned and his shorts still hung low on his hips. Her view was spectacular and the ocean had nothing to do with it. The vision of the man made her heart skip a beat involuntarily and stole her breath away yet again. Nervously, she bit her lip and tucked her hair behind her ears. Neither action distracted her. Mitchell had her full attention. And she didn't like it because she didn't want to like Mitchell Forrester.

CHAPTER TWO

'Why don't you lot come on in? The water's fine.'

Jade fought her desire to look up, but her eyes had a mind of their own and even convinced her chin to lift in the direction of the voice she knew full well was Mitchell's. It was deep and mellow, not unlike the smooth delivery of a late-night radio host on a programme that played love songs to those people who had no one beside them in bed. Jade knew the tone very well. It was how she fell asleep most nights. She had tried talk-back radio but listening to strangers' intimate thoughts didn't do anything for a good night's sleep, and the news was at times distressing, so late-night love songs became her preferred bedtime companion.

'I'm sure it is…' she started coolly, and paused as she watched through the filter of her sunglasses the water trickle down his sculpted body. She had already witnessed the firmness of the curves when he'd steadied her from tripping, but this close, and with the sun hitting every muscle and the salt water still dripping from his hair, the image was magnified. A life drawing class would not have seen a model more perfect. She tried to blink away the thoughts he was stirring but they were standing their ground and disturbing her equilibrium.

'We're happy here making sandcastles,' she finally managed to mutter with a lack of interest at his proposition she hoped was evident in her tone.

'And it's an awesome castle, but how about you and I hit the shallows?'

Jade was confused. *The shallows? Why would she want to hit the shallows?* It seemed an odd suggestion but he was being persistent and she thought it would give her the opportunity to question him over his lack of contact with his niece out of earshot of his very sweet parents. It wasn't his fault the universe had bestowed a body upon him that was causing her dormant hormones to suddenly feel alive. She would just have to deal with that. Maureen was there to take care of Amber so perhaps a stroll along the shallows would be a nice idea. The rationale for her decision to accept his proposition seemed logical, so she slowly stood to her feet. He had generously given his share of the house to Amber so her line of questioning would be polite but firm. She just had to keep her cool.

'I think that's a lovely idea,' she said, thankful that her voice did not betray her breathlessness. Now she was angry with herself as well as him.

'Great. Amber, let's go. Aunty Jade has given me approval to take you in to get your feet wet.' He stretched his hands down and playfully pulled her to her feet.

'Yippee,' came Amber's excited response, followed by a huge smile.

'Do you want to race me?'

'Yeth, I'll win!'

Jade was speechless. The invitation hadn't been for her. It had been for a splash in the shallows with his niece. Embarrassment brought the colour rushing to her cheeks as the pair took off across the sand.

'Would you like a cool drink?' Maureen asked. 'You look a little flushed. Perhaps you should come back under the umbrella with me.'

Jade nodded sheepishly and, dragging her dress in the sand, walked over to the shade where Maureen was sitting with her legs stretched out. Jade lifted her sun hat off and sat down in the soft sand. Words had escaped her. She felt like a fool but was at least grateful she'd been the only witness. It could have been worse, she thought. At least she hadn't put her hand up to be lifted from her sandy rest, so no one knew she had mistakenly thought Mitchell wanted to spend time with her.

As if he would… And as if she was interested.

It was only ever going to be a chance to hear his reason for being the absent uncle, nothing more. There was no other reason that could possibly make her want to spend time with Mitchell. Now she was doubly angry. With him…and with herself.

'Here, take this.' Maureen handed Jade a cold can of soft drink. 'It might help you to cool down.'

Jade wanted to put the icy metal can against her reddened cheeks but decided against it and drank the sweet fizzy drink instead. It felt good. And it made for a good cover. Maureen would have no idea it was pure embarrassment and not the sun that had made her blush.

'Look over there at the pair of them. Isn't he a natural father?' Maureen proudly stated rather than asked.

Jade raised her brow sceptically as she watched Mitchell and Amber splashing in the shallows. 'They're having fun,' she conceded, but she wouldn't commit to anything more. She wasn't about to agree to his paternal potential. In her eyes, he was a rolling stone who didn't show any interest in anyone but himself. Not even close to the criteria for the title of father.

'So what about you? How have you been?' Maureen asked with genuine concern and interest in her voice. 'Everything has been about Amber but what's happening in your world?'

Jade appreciated the question. It was nice to be asked but not something she had expected. 'I'm fine. Amber keeps me busy and I do part-time nursing in Neonatal ICU... I mean Intensive Care.'

'I know the acronym. Arthur's used the term enough. But it must be hard for you. Taking care of a little one and working.'

'We get by. Amber is a joy and a blessing so you'll not ever hear me complain.'

'Well, we just want you to relax and enjoy your time here. You can do with a break. I'm more than happy to help with Amber. She's so adorable and a credit to you, Jade. You've done a wonderful job, bringing her up.'

'Thank you, but it hasn't been too difficult. She's her parents' daughter and a sweetie, she rarely complains—well, except for her current dislike of broccoli and Brussels sprouts.'

'I'll remember no green vegetables when I put dinner on tonight.'

Jade returned a distracted smile as she looked back at Mitchell and Amber, now lying on the sand and letting the water hit their feet. Amber was doing her best sand angel and Jade knew her niece's toothy grin would be from ear to ear.

'Arthur told me you've applied to do some agency work while you're here. I'm more than happy, as he probably told you, to look after Amber any time. So if you want to do a shift, please, don't hesitate, but…' She paused for a moment and then her perfectly manicured hand patted Jade's, whose hands hadn't had a manicure in years. 'I just think that you, with your role as a single parent for the last three years, could do with spending the summer on the beach with a good book.'

Jade would love to do just that but she needed to work. A month without work could not be accommodated by her tight budget. While there was no mortgage, running the big house meant a lot of bills and Jade would never touch the money put away for Amber. Six months before the planned trip she had applied to the Australian Nursing and Midwifery Board for recognition of her qualification to ensure she met the criteria to allow her to work for a health professionals' agency over the month's holiday.

'I appreciate you taking care of Amber but I will try to fit my work around you and Arthur, I don't want to impose or overstep your kindness…'

'Nonsense,' Maureen countered. 'It's our pleasure and I insist that you spend the next four weeks doing whatever you want. Maybe even fit in a massage at my favourite spa. They have the most serene ambience with scented candles and soft music and I know Enrique's hands could do wonders for you.' Maureen's eyes were closed as she described the sensation.

Jade felt a tingle suddenly run down her spine. She wasn't sure if Mitchell had awakened something in her but suddenly didn't think it would be a good idea after three years of solitude to be in small softly lit room with Enrique, mood music and massage oil.

She drew a deep breath and blinked away the images.

'So…' Maureen dropped her already soft voice and leant in towards Jade '…is there a special man in your life?'

Jade was still pushing unsettling thoughts of the spa from her mind, and was about to answer the personal question diplomatically when she realised Amber was standing in front of her, dripping wet and smiling and looking a little like sand-crumbed chicken. And beside her was her very handsome beach chaperon.

Jade was painfully aware that he might have heard the question his mother had dropped on her without warning. Quickly, he confirmed her suspicions.

'Don't be shy,' Mitchell urged with a smile that showed his perfect white teeth. 'My mother is quite a busybody and if you're single she'll try to matchmake you with an eligible neighbour. So if marriage is on the cards for you and you'd like her to fix you up with an Aussie husband, let her know. Personally I couldn't think of anything worse than being trapped in that institution, but each to his, or her, own.'

Jade wasn't surprised by his views on marriage. To a man with wanderlust surging through his veins marriage would be like a prison. Ruby had been fortunate that she had met David. He had been the staying type and, no matter how short their lives had been cut by fate, they had loved each other completely. It had been a love and commitment that Jade had admired and respected but doubted she would ever find.

'I'm happily single,' she announced, not meeting Mitchell's gaze. 'And not looking for a husband here or in the US.'

Mitchell thought her answer made sense. From the way she was dressed he thought she should be singing on a hilltop in Austria. It wasn't the way a woman dressed to get a man's attention, unless he was looking for a reliable nanny for his army of children.

Jade was definitely not his type of woman. It wasn't her appearance alone that was sending him running, it was her lack of interest in anything that even slightly resembled fun. She was more like a retired army colonel than a young woman. Strict and staid.

'Well, now you know, you can leave the poor woman alone,' he told his mother with a wink that didn't go unnoticed by Jade. She wasn't sure what to make of it. Was it a signal that she was indeed a lost cause and Maureen was off the hook in trying to matchmake?

It didn't matter. Mitchell was a confirmed bachelor and she was single by choice too.

Later that evening, Mitchell and Jade found themselves sitting together after dinner on the balcony of the house. Amber and her grandparents had gone to bed early but Jade wanted to stay up a little longer to unwind from the day. Knowing Amber was safely tucked into bed, she was able to relax for the first time in many years. Finally, she had the feeling of family support and reassurance that she and Amber were not alone in the world. She knew they would only be in Adelaide for a few weeks but the love Maureen and Arthur had shown in just one day was a gift she had never expected to receive and she felt in her heart that they were forming a bond that would last a lifetime.

She didn't expect or particularly want Mitchell to stay but he did of his own choice. Maureen and Arthur had appeared exhausted from the excitement of the arrival and, Jade suspected, from the preparations for the visit.

Amber's rag doll had been washed and hung in the sun to dry, so she and her favourite doll were clean between pretty pink sheets.

Mitchell was relaxed as he swung away from the table, stretched out his tanned legs and placed them on the padded footstool. He thought the meeting with Jade and Amber had gone well. They were family and he felt good to have finally met them. Amber was a cutie and would without doubt be a heartbreaker in the future. Jade was not what he had expected but as a caregiver she fitted the bill.

He had no clue that Jade didn't feel the same way. She didn't think he fitted any bill, and she was looking for answers. With the others asleep, she decided that it was as good a time as any to get some.

She wanted Mitchell to explain his absence from Amber's life, particularly if he wanted a place in her future. But she was also mindful that his generosity in forgoing his inheritance from his brother had provided a lovely home for them. It was a little like an emotional landmine, but one she wanted to navigate to a satisfactory conclusion for all of them.

Biting the inside of her lip awkwardly, she tried to find a way to ask without the question escalating to something unpleasant, particularly in Maureen and Arthur's home. She shifted uncomfortably in her seat and drew a few short breaths. She felt a little torn about her line of approach. Gratitude, confusion and anger were all vying to direct the opening line of the conversation.

'What is it?' Mitchell asked, a little confused by her demeanour as he watched her becoming increasingly agitated.

'I just don't…' she stumbled, and paused and looked

away from his intense stare. His deep blue eyes were drawing her in. The softness of his mouth was a stark contrast to the angular lines of his jaw. The same way her demure dress was a stark contrast to the desire he was unwittingly stirring deep inside her.

The old Jade would not have hesitated to see where this infatuation might lead. To flirt a little and find out if it was a two-way street. To see if Mitchell's strong, tanned arms would pull her close and hold her as his sensual mouth claimed hers. She hurriedly blinked away the mental images that were crippling her line of thought. It was crazy. Perhaps that was a side effect of jet-lag, her sensible side suggested. But she knew the change in hemisphere wasn't bringing her to life. That it was Mitchell doing it all on his own. And she had to stop it.

Reminding herself that she didn't even like the man sitting opposite her, let alone desire him, she took a sip of her iced tea. It was old Jade's healthy but unwanted libido rising to the surface again.

'I just don't understand why you never visited Amber. She's your niece. The daughter of the brother you lost, and you didn't want to meet her. I just don't get it.' She blurted the words out at lightning speed to block out everything else she was feeling.

That was exactly the question that Mitchell had hoped to avoid. Not that it wasn't warranted. It just wasn't something he wanted to go into. He wasn't ready to once again be responsible for others. He'd been there and done that. He had hoped his financial contribution would be far more valuable than anything he could offer emotionally.

'I'm not a fan of LA,' he offered up as a reply. It was a half-truth as he didn't like big cities. 'I'm more of an uncharted waters kind of a guy. Not into multi-lane free-ways and high-rise apartments. Frankly, Hollywood just isn't my scene.'

Jade's face contorted at his response, and harshness coloured in her voice. 'She's your niece. It wasn't a sight-seeing trip that I was suggesting.'

'I'm here now,' he retorted with no audible emotion. 'Amber's a sweet little girl and I just want us to enjoy the next few weeks.'

'That still doesn't answer my question. Didn't you want to meet your brother's daughter?' Her brow was lined as she spoke. She was disappointed that he didn't offer a better explanation. She had hoped there was something of substance. Something that could justify why Mitchell had ignored his own flesh and blood for so long. But there wasn't. The long hair was gone, the beard too, but the disinterest in anything other than sat-isfying his wanderlust was still there. Jade realised that Amber would never be able to rely on her uncle and that made her sad.

Mitchell ran his long fingers through his hair ner-vously. It was clear that Jade wanted more of an expla-nation than he'd planned on providing. She would only be in town for a month. He didn't want to open up old wounds about his past and his reasons for not wanting to reach out. There was no point, he reasoned. No good would come of it. He'd been burnt, he knew his limits and that was why he steered his life away from anything that resembled long-term responsibility.

'Jade,' he began, 'I'm sorry that I couldn't be there for Amber but, in all honesty, I didn't think it would have been fair to drop in and disrupt the life she had with you and then hoist sail and take off. You provided stability for Amber. I didn't want to wreck that when I may not have been around for too long. Over the last decade, I've never stayed in one place for any length of time.'

His words were honest but they were not the entire story. He would rather appear shallow and deflect people than try to be something he wasn't and then hurt them in the long run. He just hoped that this explanation would suffice so he could leave that part of his life behind. And that part of his mother's life too. It had been sad for everyone and they were all in a better place now.

Jade wanted to hate him but the look in his eyes was somehow making that difficult. She sensed there was more to his behaviour than that, but taking a deep breath she decided that it was perhaps not the time to dig any deeper. It was late, she was tired and he had apologised. His reasons were flimsy at best but she also had to accept that losing his brother may have affected him differently. Everyone had their own way of dealing with grief. She had changed her life and settled down; Mitchell had done the opposite. Although his life on the run had started long before the accident, whatever affected Mitchell had happened well before he'd lost his brother. He clearly didn't see the world the way she did. It was best, she thought, to let it go for the time being.

Mitchell was nothing like David. And she and Amber both needed someone exactly like David. Dependable and giving with unbreakable ties to family. Mitchell didn't tick even one of those boxes. He was just a handsome drifter, a man with a wandering spirit and more than likely a wandering heart.

The night was warm and the ceiling fan was moving the air above them gently as Jade looked across the black ocean in silence. She had said enough. They both had.

The moon lit the waves as they rolled in to shore and she closed her eyes for a moment. So much had happened over the past three years. So much had changed. Three years ago she would never have thought her life would play out the way it had.

The old Jade's focus had been on living for the moment and the new Jade's was on responsibility. At times she wished her outlook on life wasn't crippled by fear, but that came with the territory of losing Ruby and David. She refused to let anything happen to Amber, ever, even if it meant wrapping her in cotton wool sometimes. It was something that Mitchell would never understand. And something she would not bother even trying to explain.

Mitchell lived in another world. And she remembered for a moment that she had once lived in a similar one. But she didn't miss it. What she had was infinitely better. She had Amber and the little girl filled her life and her heart.

As she slowly opened her eyes she felt her animosity start to lessen and looking across at Mitchell she felt it being replaced with sadness for what he had missed by not being a part of his niece's life. And for what he would miss in the future. Living the life of a rolling stone, he would never experience the joy she had every day waking up to Amber's precious face and the warmth of her cuddle.

'You've done an amazing job raising Amber,' Mitchell said, his voice husky and low and his eyes focused on hers.

Jade was taken aback by his unexpected compliment. She lowered her gaze, a little from feeling self-conscious and a little tired from the toll of a long day of travel, and graciously accepted the olive branch. 'Thank you, Mitchell.'

He poured some more iced water into their glasses and took a sip as he watched Jade sitting in the light of the moon. Unexpectedly for Mitchell, the longer he looked, the more Jade's prettiness became evident, no matter how she tried to hide it. She was cute. But not his type, he reminded himself. She was a little too serious for his liking. She was a combination of mother earth and elementary teacher with a hint of Sunday school thrown in for good measure. But he was still finding himself drawn to her and he had no idea why.

They were opposites of each other on every level. They both wanted only the best for Amber but that connection was as far as it would go. An unspoken truce was created in the warm evening breeze. Jade decided to leave the past where it belonged. And she also made a promise to herself…to leave Mitchell where he also belonged, at arm's length.

CHAPTER THREE

Within minutes of Jade's head resting back into the softness of the pillow in the bed next to Amber's she fell into a deep sleep. The past twenty-four hours had been a whirlwind. It had been happy, exhausting and a little confronting. The happiness exuded by Amber's grandparents was contagious. It was evident to anyone within a mile that Maureen and Arthur had fallen in love with Amber on sight.

Amber seemed to be enjoying the attention and being spoilt by the very kind people she had learned were her grandma and grandpa. Jade had often spoken of them over the years, and the cards and presents had arrived in the mail, but to the three-year-old they hadn't become a reality until they'd been in the same room.

The long-haul flight had been the tiring element but to Amber's credit she hadn't complained, although flying first class had made it much more enjoyable, and Jade was extremely grateful for that.

Then there was Mitchell. Meeting him had been surprisingly unsettling. She had expected so much less than the dangerously attractive windsurfer. Her mind's image of Amber's uncle had been of a scruffy, sunburnt wanderer, not unlike the survivor of a shipwreck, with hair and beard that resembled an unkempt hedge. The reality was so far removed from that. He was gorgeous and as far as she could see he was under Amber's innocent spell. But how long would that last? she wondered. Would the novelty of a niece fade as he realised that it brought with it responsibility? Although her anger was fading, her defences were still high. She accepted that he was equally irresponsible and compassionate. A walking contradiction. But no matter what, his irresponsible side would guarantee that there would be no fun excursions without her consent.

In the moments before sleep claimed her, she admitted to herself that she was suddenly experiencing emotions that she had long since packed away. Her head was spinning madly and she knew the old Jade would have stepped up and enjoyed life the way she'd known how—at full speed with no brakes and no questions. But she couldn't. Not any more. She was Amber's guardian and she knew that it required her to behave as a dependable and controlled adult, like her sister. Providing guidance and being a role model was the job description. The Jade of old had been neither. She would have been more of a warning than a role model to her niece.

Amber had to be her one and only focus. There was no room for a relationship and with a man like Mitchell a relationship would amount to one night of pleasure before he headed off to some remote location on a different continent for an indefinite period. But she dared not imagine what that night of pleasure would be like. His innocent touch sent her spiralling, so a night alone in his bed would no doubt be close to heaven.

But now she had to push those needs aside and think of someone else before herself. In her heart, Jade would always know she was the reason Amber didn't have her parents raising her so she intended to spend her life making it up to Amber.

One day, when Amber was much older, they would have that conversation. Jade hoped Amber would forgive her for sending Ruby and David away on that fateful trip. Maureen and Arthur had pleaded with Jade not to hold on to any blame when they had attended the funeral but that didn't abate the sadness and sense of responsibility she felt. She wondered if Mitchell knew the circumstances of the accident, not that she cared what he thought about her anyway. But judging by his behaviour he was not exactly strolling along any moral high road.

It didn't please Jade that Mitchell's handsome face was the last thing she pictured before she fell asleep and her first vision in the morning.

First vision?

It wasn't a dream. Jade blinked and rubbed her eyes, trying to focus. It was a reality. Mitchell was standing at the end of her bed with a beaming Amber already dressed in yet another yellow outfit, complete with a headband decorated with bumblebees and some strange blue flowers. Maureen had worked overtime in styling her granddaughter.

'Hello, Aunty Jade,' came the sweetest voice in the world. 'Here's breakfatht.'

Jade was so happy to see Amber's smiling face but equally mortified to see Mitchell. She could only guess how dishevelled she looked. Quickly, her fingers ran through her hair to straighten the bed hair catastrophe.

'Good morning, Jade,' came the radio host voice. It

wasn't forced or put on. His velvet-smooth voice was God-given.

'Good…good morning, you two. I must have slept in… What time is it?' Horror still coloured her expression.

'It's barely ten,' Mitchell said as his eyes involuntarily roamed her barely clothed body.

Pulling the bedclothes up to her chin, she sat up. She was wearing a strappy powder-blue camisole and she felt awkward and uncomfortable with Mitchell so close to her.

'I really did sleep in,' she conceded sheepishly. 'Well, I'd better get up and shower and see what Grandpa and Grandma have in mind for us today.'

'It's a pancake. I helped make it.' Her little voice was insistent.

On cue, Mitchell walked around the bed and carefully placed the tray on her lap. He paused for a moment as he looked at her, his eyes intense as they traced the curves of her body, and his mouth curved into a smile.

'Pancakes, juice and a beautiful flower too,' Jade said as she leant forward to smell the rosebud. 'I am spoilt.'

'Grandma thed that you need a retht.'

Jade smiled the most beautiful smile. That's how Mitchell saw it. In the morning light with her bed hair and skimpy nightdress he thought she looked stunning. Not prim at all. She looked naturally sexy in a girl-next-door way. He had recoiled the moment he'd put the tray on her lap. He couldn't take his eyes away from her but he didn't want her to know just how appealing he found her. He didn't want to admit it to himself either. The previous night he had taken the time to really look at Jade and try to find the woman underneath the layers of drab clothing. Now there was nothing to look past. She was in bed in something skimpy and revealing. The messy hair was so much better than the neat, slick bob. He imagined that it would be just as untidy if they had taken a motorcycle ride through the narrow, winding back roads leading through the foothills and he had slipped the passenger helmet slowly from her head before he kissed her...

He shook his head and swallowed. He had no idea what had possessed him to be thinking about the American governess like that.

'Okay, I think I'll leave you to it,' he called as he crossed the room to the doorway, quickly pulling his thoughts in line. 'I'm off to catch some waves. I intend to make the most of my last day off before I'm back at the hospital for a week straight.'

He needed to bring the unexpected images to an end. He disappeared from her sight, knowing he couldn't afford to think that way. She was off limits. Clearly, she was not his type and he was not hers. She was a sensible woman looking for a reliable nine-to-five accountant type. Not the fun-loving, fly-by-the-seat-of-your-pants sort of girl he needed. But damn, she looked so sexy all messed up in the morning.

Jade watched him leave the room, not knowing what he was thinking. But she definitely had unwanted thoughts about the man who had brought her breakfast in bed.

She enjoyed the wonderful spread as she listened to Amber's adventures in the kitchen, cooking pancakes. She felt a little guilty that Amber had never enjoyed time with her extended family before now. But she conceded that it hadn't been possible before. Amber's health had

had to take precedence. Maureen and Arthur had never said the trip would be too difficult emotionally for them but their lack of travel to Los Angeles spelt it out to Jade and she understood. Burying their son was the only memory they had of the city. And Jade had been busy trying to pay the bills and monitoring Amber's medical issues while working part time, so a trip Down Under hadn't been a priority, but she decided, as she was listening to her niece's tales from the morning, that this trip should not be the last.

When her plate and glass were empty, Jade slipped on her long cotton dressing gown and the two of them made their way downstairs so Jade could say good morning and thank Maureen for a delicious breakfast. After a chat over a cup of coffee, Maureen and Arthur offered to take Amber for a stroll along the jetty to see if they could spot any dolphins, have lunch and give Jade some much-needed time to herself. Amber was excited by the idea so Jade agreed. Amber had taken to her grandparents and Jade was very happy.

'I thought we might have a little birthday party dinner for Amber tonight,' Maureen said softly so that Amber couldn't hear.

'But her birthday isn't for three days.'

'I know, but Mitchell will be working all week and he always works late, and I thought it would be lovely for him to be a part of the celebrations.'

'Whatever you would like to do.'

'We can have a little luncheon party on the day at the zoo perhaps but this is a pre-birthday party, and it means Amber will get two cakes this year!'

Again Jade wasn't about to say no. It was Maureen's decision; it made her happy and it appeared to have been made already. Jade was aware that this week would be particularly hard on all of them. It was the third anniversary of the accident. It had been a day that had changed everyone's lives for ever. Those who'd died, the one who had been born and the ones who'd been robbed of loved ones. So a double celebration of Amber's birthday would be a distraction that would be beneficial for everyone.

'There's lots of salad things in the refrigerator and some lovely fresh bread on the bench,' Maureen announced on the way out the door. 'Please, help yourself for lunch, unless, of course, you want to join us. You're most welcome—we don't want you to think we've kidnapped Amber but we do feel that you've being doing it alone for so long that you should have a break.'

'I think I will stay in, but thank you for the invitation. Salad sounds great.'

Alone in the house, Jade decided to enjoy a swim in the pool. The only 'old Jade' outfit she had packed was a nude-coloured string bikini. She never had time to go swimming back home between work and Amber so it was the one piece of clothing she hadn't bothered to replace with something a little more sensible. A little more suitable for her role as Amber's guardian. Knowing that the house was hers, she slipped on the tiny swimsuit and, feeling a little self-conscious, wrapped a towel around herself and made her way to the pool, where she planned on doing laps of the crystal water in solitude.

The solar heating had taken the chill off, rendering it refreshing but not cold. Jade swam the length of the pool on her back, looking at the clear blue sky with not a cloud in sight. The morning sun was warm and the breeze had dropped. It was a perfect day and she was enjoying the feeling of the water against her near-naked body.

The last time she had felt so uninhibited had been on a holiday in Cabo San Lucas almost four years before. It seemed a lifetime ago. Not that she would trade her life or anyone in it but she was relishing a few minutes to herself. She climbed out of the water and, still wet, lay down on the sun lounge. Her skin was a light golden colour courtesy of one of her nurse friends who had insisted on giving Jade a spray tan in her home before she'd left for Australia.

'Don't want the Aussies to tread on you 'cos you match the white sand,' her friend had said with a laugh as she'd refilled the airbrushing machine while Amber had sat giggling as she'd watched. They had covered the room with plastic bags to protect the white tiles from the brown stain. It had been a fun afternoon, and Amber thought they'd been quite silly and very messy.

Mitchell let himself into the house. With the car gone, he assumed his parents and the house guests had headed off somewhere for the day. The beach had been great, not yet hot and with just enough of a breeze for him to enjoy an hour's windsurfing before he dropped his gear back at his house. It had cooled his libido as well.

Seeing Jade in bed, looking so dishevelled, had made him view her differently and that was wrong. He knew when she was put back together the way she apparently liked to dress, she would not be his type. He liked to spend his time with fun-loving, easygoing women who knew the rules. No strings attached and definitely no schoolmarm attire. He just wanted a good time and he never misled a woman about it. He called it as it was and the women he dated knew he was not husband material.

There was no chance of Mitchell Forrester being tied down. Long-term relationships always brought responsibility in buckets and he knew he was certain to fail if he was pushed to travel that road again. There was nothing that would convince him otherwise. He was burnt out on that level. He had been bolting at the first sign of responsibility or commitment in his personal life for more than a decade and he had no intention of changing now. And Jade had commitment written all over her conservative self.

Walking in the front door in his now dry board shorts and sans a top, the house was quiet, just as he'd imagined it would be. Amber was as cute as could be but her high-pitched chatter with a distinct American accent would probably not let him concentrate on the task at hand. He loved children and that was why he had specialised in neonatology and paediatrics but he liked to keep his private life and his professional life separate. He never planned on having children of his own. The title of father did not factor into his future. Uncle was fine but that would be his limit.

He spied the new sound system that Arthur had purchased lying unopened in the box in the living room. Arthur had no idea of how to actually make it work, and Mitchell had offered to connect it. With an empty house, he knew he would have the job finished quickly. With Maureen around, any job he did for them resembled an instructional video on replay as she asked a barrage of questions with each step he took and then asked him to repeat it again later. So this chore would be a pleasant change. He would have it all done and be gone before they came home, and that sat well with him.

Leaving before they pulled into the driveway would be best. It wasn't that he didn't want to see Amber, it was more that he didn't know if he wanted to see Jade. She was a conundrum. The morning before he'd felt positive that he could be around her and not feel at all attracted. But that morning when she'd lain in her crumpled bed, all fresh-faced and messy, she'd suddenly inched a little closer to being his type. And that was a bad thing.

Maybe that was the real Jade. He wondered if the new Jade was an attempt to be more like Ruby. A woman invented to be what Ruby and David would have wanted.

But lying in bed she had been exactly what he wanted. He pushed the image from his mind. There was work to do and daydreaming about Jade would not progress anything except his desire to a level requiring a cold shower.

Mitchell cut open the box and removed the first speaker. All he needed to start was the tool kit from the shed by the pool.

Jade had finished applying the sunscreen to her body. The mid-morning sun probably wouldn't burn but she knew that underneath her man-made tan she was still naturally pale and was aware the Australian sun was quite intense. With her skin now glistening from the lotion, she lay back on the sun lounge to enjoy the warm rays. Her oversized sunglasses protected her eyes and her earphones were plugged in. She didn't have to listen out for Amber for a few hours, so she listened to her favourite southern rock as she lay in the warm sun. She didn't have to hide as there was no one to see her in the private pool area. Her bikini was still wet and her skin tone was now a perfect match. She was completely un-aware that from twenty or more feet away she appeared to be completely naked.

Mitchell spied Jade from the corner of his eye and dropped the entire contents of the tool kit on the ground. His chiselled jaw fell and his eyes widened as he saw the most stunning vision lying naked beside the pool.

Jade?

It couldn't be her...or could it?

He hadn't seen her when he'd walked to the shed and rifled through the contents, looking for a screw-driver and small wrenches. It had been as he'd closed the shed door that he'd seen her body draped across the sun lounge. He had never seen a woman so perfect. And she was naked. That made the vision doubly perfect to him.

He struggled to pull his eyes away. The desire to ad-mire her stunning body was fighting with the shreds of decency that had survived the shock of seeing her like that. Falling to his knees and not allowing himself to look in her direction, he began gathering the tools now strewn across the pavers leading back to the house. It was obvious she hadn't seen him so he decided to exit the back yard and go inside without causing her any em-barrassment. She had obviously decided to skinny-dip while the family were out, he realised as he fumbled to collect the last tool that had rolled onto the lawn.

But Jade skinny-dipping?

That was not in keeping with the persona she was portraying to everyone. She had gone from looking like a missionary to a centrefold. Maybe this was the real Jade. The woman his brother had called the rebel sister

was lying naked under the Australian sun. He liked this
Jade so much more.

His heart was pulsing blood around his body at an
alarming rate. His mind was spinning with the image
that he didn't want to blink away. The idea that Jade
was prim and uptight no longer had any grounds for
existence. Jade was so far from what she hid beneath
her dowdy clothing. Clothing that he now suspected
was a shield from the world or a reaction to what had
happened. When his brother had died, he had run further from responsibility and Jade, he now assumed, had
stepped up, left the fun behind and donned the sensible
clothing. She had morphed into her sensible sister, Ruby.

Without making another sound or looking back, he
left. He had stumbled upon the most beautiful vision
but he wasn't about to take advantage of the situation.
Jade thought she was alone and he would respect that
assumption and leave the house. There was no need for
him to let her know that he had accidentally seen what
she hid from the rest of the world. The sound system
had to wait until another day. Mitchell needed to take a
plunge in the ocean to cool off.

Jade lowered her sunglasses. Over the music, she thought
she heard a noise. It was like a door was being slammed.
She pulled the earphones free, wrapped the towel around
her damp bikini and headed inside.

'Anyone home?'

No response came back so, surmising it had probably been a neighbour's door, she headed upstairs for
a warm shower. The swim and the sun had been wonderful beyond belief, but she had calls to make. She
needed to let the nursing agency know she had arrived

and was ready for work as she needed an income while she was in Adelaide. It was obvious that Amber loved being with her grandparents and they adored being with her, so a weight had lifted from her, and Jade knew she wouldn't be putting anyone out by working some shifts at a local hospital.

She was waiting for jet-lag to hit but it hadn't so she suspected she might be one of the few who didn't suffer the effects from long-haul flights. So she was ready to start working whenever they called. Her papers were in order, she had been approved by the statutory body and she was ready to take on whatever temporary nursing was available.

Mitchell dived into the cool waves and intended on swimming until the image of Jade lying naked on the sun lounge began to fade. Around two hundred strokes into his swim he realised that it would never disappear. It was burnt into his memory. And he wasn't entirely sure he wanted to erase it. It was much too stunning a visual to give up that easily. He would just try very hard not to recall it too often.

And particularly not when she was near him.

Jade put her damp swimsuit in the laundry to dry and dressed in a calf-length grey-and-white striped skirt and grey knit top then put a call in to the nursing agency. While she was waiting to hear back, she towel-dried her hair as she wandered around the stunning home. There were pictures of David and Mitchell everywhere. As children, teenagers and also their graduation photos complete with caps, gowns and scrolled parchment.

Maureen was obviously very proud of her sons and

their achievements and Arthur was an equally proud stepfather. Jade didn't know what had happened to their biological father but she did recall David saying that he had been quite young when his parents had divorced and Arthur had married Maureen quite a few years later. Then she spied Maureen and Arthur's wedding photograph. Maureen looked to be in her early forties and Arthur perhaps in his late forties. They were dressed quite simply, both in suits, and the photograph had been taken in a park rotunda with a marriage celebrant.

A photo at the back, almost hidden from view, then took her attention. It was of a very young Mitchell dressed in a work uniform. He looked barely old enough to be in high school but he was in what appeared to be a large warehouse. He appeared far too young to be working. Perhaps it had been work experience, she thought as she put down the photograph.

She noticed there were a few photographs of Mitchell, resembling Tarzan, on his travels, although none with women, as there had been in the photos he had sent David. Instead, they were all solo shots in the wilderness. He had hidden his array of girlfriends from his mother, which did hint at a level of good taste. She quickly blinked away thoughts of his very active love life and continued admiring the collections of photographs.

There were pictures from the beach wedding of David and Ruby. Jade reached down and picked up one of the silver-framed photographs. The happy couple were beaming and the beach at sunset in the background was spectacular. She ran her finger absent-mindedly over the image of her sister. Her long blonde hair was braided with fresh flowers and the hemline of her stunning white lace wedding gown disappeared into the sand. Ruby was a beautiful bride and they looked such a happy couple. Jade put the frame down with a tear threatening to spill onto her cheek.

She noticed pictures of Amber on the sideboard and the sight of them all lifted her mood. So many of the photographs that Jade had sent to them were on display, and each had its own frame.

Maureen and Arthur were doting grandparents.

Jade's mobile phone suddenly rang in the pocket of her skirt.

'Hello, Jade Grant,' she answered, after pulling it free.

'Hi, Jade, this is Susy from the ANR agency. We spoke earlier and I wanted to see if you would consider a three-week placement, starting tomorrow.'

'That's quick, but, yes, I'm sure it will be fine,' Jade responded, immediately recognising the acronym for the Australian Nursing Recruitment Agency. She had thought it would be a few days till she heard anything from them.

'With your experience and your qualifications in neo-natal ICU and midwifery, you were snapped up. I only wish you could stay longer. There would never be a shortage of work for you,' Susy told her. 'I know you only want to work part time during your stay in Adelaide so this placement is three shifts per week. It's to cover holidays and I have another temp neonatal nurse who can job-share with you. What do you think?'

'I think it sounds great. Where will I be working?'

'You'll be at the Eastern Memorial right in the heart of Adelaide, working across paediatrics and neonatal as I know you have experience in both. I think you'll like working there. The nursing staff are second to none, the facilities state of the art.'

'It sounds wonderful.'

After Jade ended the call she turned away from the photos of the family and breathed a sigh of relief. It was hard to admit it, but she had to concede that Mitchell was beyond attractive and he had stirred some feelings she'd forgotten she had ever felt, but now this would not be an issue: she would be busy working three days a week so would not see much of him during her stay.

Despite his obvious masculine appeal, and the way he was making her feel, she tried to convince herself that Mitchell Forrester would not be a threat to her. He was wayward and reckless if his postcards were anything to go by, she told herself just in case her hormones were making their own plans. Reliable, steadfast and sensible would be the prerequisites for any man to be in Amber's life, just the way Ruby had liked her men. And it wouldn't happen for a very long time, if ever. She needed to focus on being the best caregiver to Amber. That was the role she had been given and she intended on doing the very best job.

She had sat Amber down a few months before the trip and tried to explain why her life was different.

'I know that most of your friends at playgroup have mommies and daddies but you have an aunty instead,' Jade began to explain. 'Your mommy and daddy look down from heaven and watch over you every day to make sure you are happy and safe. And I think that I am the luckiest aunty in the world to have you.'

Jade had become Amber's legal guardian with Maureen and Arthur's blessing as they had wanted what was best for their granddaughter. Mitchell had never contested the role, and Jade wasn't surprised. Jade had seen from the moment she'd arrived in Adelaide that nothing had changed. Maureen and Arthur were so supportive and Mitchell was just there for the fun times.

'Ith it my birthday?' Amber squealed her question when she saw her grandfather blowing up balloons and her grandmother putting out pink and yellow napkins and a small stack of brightly wrapped gifts on the table.

'Not for a few days, but this is an early birthday party so that Uncle Mitchell can say happy birthday and watch you blow out the candles,' Maureen told her. 'He has to go to work for the rest of the week so he will miss your real birthday. So you'll have two parties.'

Amber's eyes grew wider. 'Two parties?'

'Yes, Amber,' Jade answered. 'Grandma is spoiling you and you'll be having two parties this year.'

Amber was clapping her hands and laughing as she sat beside her grandfather while he blew up the last of the balloons.

'Don't tell me I'm doing this again in a few days?'

'Darling,' Maureen began, 'there's only a handful of balloons so please just tie the ribbons onto each one and we can put them up before Mitchell arrives.'

'Too late, I'm here.'

Mitchell had initially hesitated to accept the dinner invitation when his mother had called but when he'd discovered it was to celebrate Amber's birthday he agreed immediately. The vision of Jade by the pool had haunted him all day and was the reason he'd hesitated. Something made him want to stay away from Jade but something stronger made him want to spend time with her.

He wanted to find out more about her, and if he was right about her motives. Did she really think that wearing clothes so dour that they were suited to a retired prison warden would make her a better guardian? A blind man could see her devotion and success raising Amber. She didn't need to dress in costume to achieve anything. He would never understand why she covered the body he knew for a fact was amazing. And why she seemed so averse to his light-hearted remarks about life.

It was as if she had nominated herself for the position of moral compass of the family, if not the world. But as he looked at her he had to admit something about her was growing on him. She was cute, a good and devoted woman, and now that he had seen so much more she had also become desirable woman in his eyes. Common sense told him to limit his time around her but something else told him the opposite.

Jade turned around to see Mitchell standing in the doorway with a large white bear in a yellow spotted dress and a very small white box with a silver bow. He was wearing black jeans, black boots and a tight plain white T-shirt that didn't hide his ample chest. She felt her temperature start to rise and her heart flutter. Then she noticed he was avoiding eye contact with her.

She prayed he had not seen her watching him from her balcony as he'd walked to the beach that morning. The swagger in his step and his lean, tanned body barely dressed had had a mind-numbing effect on her the moment she'd seen him and the image was still close to doing the same now. She felt her skin heat up and threaten to flush and she was bewildered by what was happening to her.

Over the past three years on her own she must have seen hundreds of good-looking men walking the streets, having coffee in the hospital cafeteria, in the twenty-four-hour supermarket when she called in after a late shift, but none of them had stirred any interest. Nothing.

She'd walked past them as if they'd been store manne-quins. But now, looking at Mitchell, she was very aware of the unsettling attraction she was feeling.

With difficulty, she attempted to drag her thoughts back to where they belonged and where they needed to remain for the next few weeks.

'This is for the birthday girl,' Mitchell said, his hands outstretched to Amber.

Jade could see Amber's face light up as Arthur led her by the hand over to Mitchell and the presents.

'The teddy is for now,' he began, as he put the bear into her arms. 'And this present is for when you are older.' He carefully handed her the small present.

Jade noted the colour of the dress. Mitchell had re-membered Amber's favourite colour. Amber took the presents and gave Mitchell a hug before she returned to the chair and unwrapped the white bow on the box, her teddy firmly planted on her little lap.

'It-th's pretty!' she exclaimed, as she pulled a silver heart-shaped locket from the box. 'Look, Aunty Jade, it-th's pretty.'

'You can put photos inside so one day when you are off travelling the world you will always have your fam-ily travelling with you,' Mitchell added.

Amber had no idea what he was talking about but Jade was taken aback and the expression on her face did not hide it. The teddy was cute and the locket was lovely but the message behind it didn't sit well with her. *Was this Mitchell's advice to her?* Head off, put fam-ily in a locket and live your life somewhere else? She hadn't pictured Amber ever leaving to see the world. She felt sick at the thought of not being there to protect her. And upset that Mitchell was using Amber's birthday to impart his set of values on niece when she was only three years old.

'That is very pretty' she said, as she sat down and opened the delicate locket. 'It will be lovely to wear to very special *parties*.' Not a trip around the world away from family, she continued in her mind.

'I'm surprised you didn't buy one in green to go with her camouflage outfit for her trip down the Amazon for her sixth birthday,' she said to Mitchell in a lowered voice as she made her way past him to the kitchen. 'Really, a trip around the world? She's three years old and maybe there's the chance she'll be like her father and she won't want to run away from her family.'

Mitchell was stunned into silence. He thought her rebuke was an overreaction. It was a present of his choice with his sentiment. Not everyone saw the world the way Jade obviously did. He noted her dress sense had returned to that of elderly maiden aunt.

'Like me? Is that what you mean? Actually, the message was about the importance of family,' he said in the same low voice with a scowl as he followed her into the kitchen. 'Pity you couldn't see past your own agenda to see I didn't have one.'

'My agenda?'

'Yes. It's pretty obvious you're planning on wrapping Amber in cotton wool for her entire life. Let her build sandcastles but avoid the water. Like a bystander who can watch but not experience life. That's what this is about. It's not healthy to bring up a child with no sense of adventure.'

'How lovely to see you two getting to chat finally,' Maureen said as she entered the kitchen to collect some plates. 'Arthur is putting some prawns on the barbeque to go with the potato bake and salad.'

'That sounds delicious,' Jade said through gritted teeth. She was so angry with Mitchell. She was just protecting her niece the best way she knew how. She suddenly prayed that Mitchell wasn't right. She didn't want to cocoon Amber and not let her take her place in the world or have fun as she grew up. She bit her lip as her eyes darted nervously around the room. His words made her question herself. *Was she at risk of smothering Amber?*

'I'll see what I can do to help outside,' Mitchell said, his eyes narrowing in Jade's direction before he disappeared onto the balcony to help Arthur put up the balloons.

'Such a pretty locket and so sweet of Mitchell to think of something like that. I thought you'd approve of something so delicate and timeless,' Maureen said as she collected the salad from the refrigerator, added some home-made dressing and headed back outside.

'Very pretty,' Jade returned. She couldn't agree with the rest of Maureen's words. She wasn't sure what she thought about Mitchell or herself any more.

Mitchell and Jade chose to sit at opposite ends of the table for dinner. They said nothing to each other and neither made eye contact with the other. Amber didn't appear to have much of an appetite and just played with her food, then lay down on the sofa with her new teddy.

'Are you okay, sweetheart?' Jade asked with a little frown of concern.

'I'm full.'

Maureen looked over at Amber and lowered her voice. 'She didn't want much for lunch today either. I think jet-lag has hit her. It was a long trip for a little girl. And you too, Jade.'

'I'll keep an eye on it,' Jade said. 'You're probably right but if she doesn't pick up I'll take her for a check-up.'

'Do you want me to make an appointment with the nephrologist just for peace of mind?' Arthur asked. 'It's probably not related but it will put your mind at rest.'

'Let's see how she goes,' Jade replied, as she watched Amber play with her yet-to-be named bear. 'The flight probably exhausted her. In a day or so she should pick up.'

'Teddy wants to lie down, he'th tired.' Amber said softly.

The adults all smiled and returned to their dinner, each of them not wanting to appear concerned but still keeping an eye on Amber.

'And what did you get up to today while Amber was showing us the dolphins, Jade?' Maureen finally asked to lift the conversation.

'Nothing much... I just relaxed by the pool.'

Mitchell choked loudly on hearing the words. His drink threatened to spill from his lips and his eyes watered as he valiantly fought to not splutter. *Nothing much* didn't just describe her day...it did, however, describe her outfit, or lack thereof, perfectly. She had been lying naked by the pool. And had looked amazing doing so.

'Are you all right, dear?'

'Uh-huh,' he responded, his lips forming a rueful slant as he tried not to make eye contact with Jade. He wasn't all right. He wanted to be honest and tell her that he had seen her that morning lying sans clothing by the water's edge but he would never embarrass her that way. Also peeping Tom came to mind to describe him and he didn't want that label. It had been an accidental sighting but a very pleasant one.

But the sighting even now, many hours later, was

causing his heart to beat a little faster despite his opinion of her. It was an image at total odds with the role she was playing. Perhaps being the only one at the table who knew the real Jade drew him to her. He had seen the version she was hiding from the world and his parents. And he liked what he'd seen. He suspected why she was behaving that way but he didn't agree with it. Just as she had over-reacted about the locket, Jade was trying to protect her niece from the world and even the real Jade. He just had to find a way to convince her that she didn't need to be anything other than herself.

'I just got a bit of sun…'

'Oh, I'd say you got a whole lot of sun,' he muttered under his breath.

'Is everything okay?' she asked with a curious frown.

'Yes, fine, I'm just saying that you must have enjoyed sunbathing while everyone was out. I guess you just *really* like the sun.'

'What a peculiar thing to say, Mitchell,' Maureen said as she took another mouthful of salad.

Jade shot him a confused glance as she collected the plates.

'Never mind,' Mitchell returned as he stood to take the stack of plates from Jade's hands. His warm skin brushed against hers and the electricity surged despite her anger towards him.

'Forget I said anything. It's just my warped Aussie humour. I'm sorry if the present upset you. There was nothing meant by it. Amber can put anything she wants in the locket. By the time she's sixteen she will probably have a crush on a pop star who can't sing a note but he'll have great hair and perfect teeth and she will put his picture in the locket.'

Jade stepped into the kitchen. 'More than likely.' Her tone was cool but pleasant.

'What about a truce?' he whispered as he followed her. 'For Amber's sake?'

Jade met his glance but wasn't convinced.

'I was out of line,' he apologised. 'I understand you want to keep Amber safe. With what happened to Ruby and David, you have every right. But please trust me, I would never let anything happen to Amber.'

Jade squinted a little as she took his words on board. They did seem heartfelt and she didn't want any animosity ruining what little time they had with Maureen and Arthur.

'Truce.'

'Happy birthday, dear Amber, happy birthday to you.'

Amber was happy to sit back at the table for the arrival of her two-tier princess birthday cake. Her eyes lit up when she saw the iced strawberry sponge cake with tiny wax figurines of her favourite storybook princesses sitting on the top, with three candles burning brightly.

To the sounds of *Hip, hip, hooray*, she blew out the candles, ate half of the slice of cake on her plate and then went back to the sofa with her new teddy and rag doll. The trip had taken its toll, and Jade wasn't surprised that Amber wanted to go to bed early.

On seeing how tired she was, Mitchell scooped her up and carried her to the bathroom, where Jade brushed her teeth then slipped her into her pyjamas before he helped to tuck her into bed.

His assistance with the bedtime preparations was his effort to show he was serious about the truce and helping out, but he was surprised how much he enjoyed being a part of it all. Something deep inside felt good about being able to kiss Amber on the forehead and hear her say goodnight to him. It was a long way from his handshake two days previously. He had never experienced that unconditional affection.

He spent all of his working hours saving the lives of children but he never saw them tucked into their own beds. He experienced gratitude in buckets from the parents, although he never expected it. Ensuring these little patients had the best possible opportunity for healthy, happy lives was just what he did. But as he stood watching Amber drift off to sleep he felt a tug at his heart. Perhaps he was missing out on something after all.

He wondered for a moment if his self-imposed exile from family and commitment was worth it.

Then he shook his head and realised that he was fooling himself.

Despite his feelings towards his niece, he would never be ready for children and a family full time, it wasn't in his genes.

'Are you okay to sleep in here by yourself for a little while?' Jade asked softly. 'I'll leave the door open and you can hear us on the balcony.'

Amber nodded and she went to sleep with her bear and rag doll. She was so tired she didn't need a story. Jade couldn't help but notice the shift in Mitchell and how his face had lit up when Amber had said goodnight to him.

'I've been asked to start tomorrow for the temp agency,' Jade announced on their way back to the dinner table. 'I have a three-week placement.'

'That's great. Which hospital?' Mitchell asked as he tried to process the feelings that still lingered after being a part of Amber's bedtime ritual.

'The Eastern Memorial,' she said, then added, 'Arthur told me it was his old workplace.'

'Yes, it was,' Mitchell replied with a rueful look. But he didn't tell her that it was also his workplace and that he was a consultant neonatologist there.

And that fate had just decreed that he would be her very temporary boss.

CHAPTER FOUR

MITCHELL WALKED DOWN to the water's edge in the warm night air. He wanted to clear his head before he tried to sleep. This was not how he had seen Jade and Amber's visit playing out. He had pictured a fun-loving, easygoing woman, a kindred spirit of sorts. A Californian beach babe who might like to hang out, enjoy a few drinks at a bar, hit the surf and maybe even enjoy a casual hook-up.

Instead, he had found a woman whose commitment ran so much deeper than that. She had changed everything about her life for her niece. In Mitchell's eyes it wasn't necessary and he doubted he would be able to do the same, but he couldn't help but admire how far she would go to provide the upbringing she believed her niece needed.

The rebel girl was now more at home having a cup of tea and an early night on her own. And she would give her life to protect Amber but he found it such a waste for her to hide behind the image of someone else. He had seen the real woman beside the pool and it had sent his body into overdrive.

She was pretending to be so much less than she was. Looking out over the moonlit water, Mitchell wondered how someone could be so completely selfless. Someone so young and beautiful who would have so many options yet she had obviously turned her back on them all for Amber.

He wanted to know more about her yet he had to prevent this conundrum of a woman from getting under his skin. He didn't want to be involved with a woman that genuine. It would be a disaster for everyone. The idea of being tied to one woman and having a family would never work for him. Or would it? he wondered as he picked up a pebble and cast it into the moonlit ocean. It had felt so good to be in the room with Jade, putting Amber to bed. It had seemed so natural and as if they had done it before…and could do it a thousand times and never tire of it.

But there was doubt weighing heavily in his mind. An uncertainty that he could stay the course. A hesitation in his heart that he could not be relied on in a forever situation. His greatest misgiving would be his ability to last the distance and not break the hearts of those who loved him.

Until now that had never been tested. Until now he had never wanted to really get to know a woman beyond a one-night stand or contemplate being a part of a woman's life.

The feelings that he was experiencing were all new to him. Mitchell was at an unexpected crossroad with no clue how he intended on navigating his future.

He stood in silence alone on the beach more confused than he had ever been.

Jade crossed to the scrub room and slipped on a disposable gown over the white nursing uniform she had pulled from her suitcase and pressed that morning. Morning had come quickly after another good night's sleep. Amber's day had been so filled with fun and adventure with her grandparents and then her early birthday dinner that she had been exhausted and had slept through the night, allowing Jade to do the same.

Jade's shift began at two in the afternoon and she would finish at ten that night. Arthur had offered to drive her but Jade had insisted on catching the tram as the temp agency had advised, since their home was not far from the tram stop on Jetty Road. She really didn't want to impose and it gave her a chance to see more of the city on her walk.

She reached out with her foot to the pedal to turn on the tap and noticed a woman in her late twenties, with a worried expression and dressed in a gown and slippers, drying her hands. Jade gave her an encouraging smile.

'I hope to be going home soon. It's my third day,' the woman said softly, returning a meek smile. 'I so wish I was taking Jasper with me but that will be a while, they say. How long do prem babies usually stay in hospital?'

'It's hard to say because all babies are different,' Jade began to explain. 'It depends on how your baby's progressing. Babies who are smaller and those born earlier sometimes have some medical problems other than just being tiny and so tend to stay longer on the unit. But a premature baby who is otherwise well usually stays in the neonatal unit until around the date he or she was due to be born. If your baby does very well, is eating and gaining weight, then he or she might even be able go home even sooner. How early was Jasper?'

'Ten weeks early. He's on a ventilator because he has a lung problem that I don't really understand,' she returned quietly. 'Hy-mem…something disease. The doctor tried to explain it to me but I didn't really understand. And I didn't want to ask too many questions. I thought he might think I'm being pushy, wanting to know everything medical when I'm not a doctor or even think I'm stupid for not understanding.'

Jade knew from her training and years of neonatal nursing that mothers of premature babies and their families all faced uncertainty and this caused raised levels of anxiety. Visiting their baby in Neonatal Intensive Care was a stressful situation that most knew little or nothing about.

'It's important that you never think of yourself as being difficult. Any questions you might have are valid,' Jade explained, as she turned off the tap with her elbow. She was aware that the exchange of information allowed the nurses to gauge the stress within the family and most particularly the mother's ability to cope. 'Parents need to feel a part of the decisions being made for their baby, and you can't do that if you don't understand what is happening.'

'Really? He won't mind if I keep asking questions, and he won't think they're silly things I'm asking? It's just that you're here every day and it's all so new to me.'

'I promise you that the doctors and the nursing staff would never think of any questions as silly. More than likely the doctor assumed that you knew what he was saying if you didn't ask any questions, and I guarantee he would have been more than happy to explain it to you. You're a mother of a newborn in intensive care and you have every right and need to know what is happening throughout his treatment. Please, never hesitate to ask any of us whatever you want to know.'

The young woman sighed and seemed to lift in confidence a little.

'I just don't know what the disease is and why Jasper has it?'

'Hyaline membrane disease is also called infant respiratory distress syndrome and is suffered by almost half of premature babies under thirty weeks,' Jade offered instinctively as the woman's body language showed she was relaxing. 'It means that every time Jasper breathes in he has to expand his lungs completely. Healthy lungs don't collapse to an airless state, but because of his prematurity Jasper's lungs are deflating totally. It makes breathing very hard work for him.'

The woman dropped the dampened paper towel into the bin and tentatively approached Jade, looking for reassurance. 'So it's common, then?'

'Many premature babies have issues with breathing as a result of their early arrival, and even if they aren't as premature as Jasper they can still have this problem. But your baby is in very good hands here. If you have any questions about Jasper and the doctor isn't available, just ask any of the nurses.'

'I haven't seen you here before. You're American. Have you moved to Adelaide to live?'

'No, I'm on a working holiday. Today is my first shift and I will be here for the next three weeks. So let me know if you have any other questions. I'll be here tonight till late.'

'Thanks so much. I have to express some milk and grab something to eat. The nurse told me that I have to keep up my calories to make sure I can produce enough for Jasper.'

Jade nodded. 'Yes, you do. You have to get sleep and

rest and eat well for both you and Jasper. One of the most important things you and your partner can do for your baby is look after yourselves. Get sleep, eat healthy meals, and take a break from it all. It's exhausting having a baby in the neonatal unit, particularly after a difficult or emergency birth. It's natural to want to put your baby first but you must be good to yourself, too.'

She watched as the woman put a half-smile on her tired face then left the washroom to head back to the ward, hopefully secure in the knowledge that she could ask anything she needed to know without any judgement from the medical staff. Ultimately, she would be her baby's only constant in the multiple care-giving system of neonatal intensive care and she needed to feel confident in that role.

Jade had already been given her patient roster at handover. It wasn't a busy time in the nursery and she only had two infants to monitor. Checking the first infant's chart, she noted that Costa was due for a gavage feed. She crossed slowly to another nurse already on duty. As she drew closer, she noticed she was quite young. She had a friendly face with a smattering of freckles across the bridge of her nose. Her hair was a mass of copper curls kept out of her eyes with a pearly clasp on the top of her head. She wasn't particularly tall, perhaps two or three inches shorter than Jade, and this added to her overall young appearance. She imagined that Amber might look similar when she was older.

'Hi, I'm Jade.'

'I'm Mandy. You're from the agency too, then?'

'Yes, first shift and staying for about three weeks, part time, though.'

'Welcome on board.' Then, distracted by something

or someone in the glass-walled scrub room, she paused and then lowered her voice. 'Scrumptious, isn't he?'

Jade noticed a huge smile spread across the young nurse's face but had no idea why.

'If I wasn't engaged…' Mandy began in a wistful tone, before tilting her head to one side in the direction of the door '… I'd offer him breakfast in bed.'

'Who?' Jade cut in.

'Mitchell Forrester, the dishy doctor just scrubbing in.'

Jade froze. Mitchell worked at the hospital? He hadn't mentioned it the night before. She felt her stomach jump and her heart race. *Why hadn't he told her?* She was suddenly quite confused as she'd thought they were getting on well and if he wanted it to remain that way he certainly should have volunteered that information the previous night.

Perhaps he didn't like the idea of them working together. She couldn't be sure but there were so many things about which she wasn't sure. Including her feelings for the man scrubbing in. She could see exactly why the nurse spoke that way. Mitchell was very handsome and more than likely up for some fun with the right woman, but it wasn't her. She was not in the market for a one-night stand and up until now her resolve to stay single had not been tested.

'I suppose,' Jade replied coldly, not wanting to let on that she had any connection to Mitchell or the fact there was a tiny part of her that agreed.

'It doesn't hurt to have some eye candy in the workplace. I mean, it's a nice distraction from the round-the-clock care we provide for premmies. I think it's the universe rewarding us!'

Jade could not join her enthusiasm. She wanted to be anywhere else but near Mitchell. He was resurrecting needs she had put to rest the moment Amber had arrived in her life. She didn't want or need a distraction from her role. She didn't dare let her eyes rest on him for long. His raw masculinity was reminding her that she was a woman with desires that hadn't been met in a very long time.

'I guess, from what I've heard, the parents can rest assured their babies are in the very best hands. And in Mitchell Forrester's hands is where I'm sure every second nurse in the hospital would like to be,' she added with a laugh.

'Well, there's no accounting for taste,' Jade answered woodenly, making it clear she had no intention of joining the recruitment line for his harem. Then she noticed that a theatre nurse spoke to him briefly and he turned and left the scrub room with her.

She was relieved that he wasn't coming in. It gave her a little longer without him there.

Her attention quickly returned to baby Costa. She began the gavage feed that was due by aspirating the contents of his tiny stomach to assess the quantity of still undigested food, along with the colour and appearance. Satisfied that everything was within normal limits, Jade slowly returned the contents to ensure that valuable electrolytes were not lost. Then, attaching the syringe with the milk, she held it above the baby to allow gravity to control the feed, and began the thirty-minute process.

'I'm Soula, Costa's mum,' came a young female voice as Jade was about twenty minutes into the feed.

Jade raised her eyes only momentarily from her tiny

patient to acknowledge the young woman dressed in her gown and slippers.

'Hello, Soula. I'm Jade, and I'll be looking after Costa this afternoon. He's certainly a handsome young man.'

'He looks like his father,' Soula returned with a nervous smile. 'The same thick black hair. His *yia-yia*, Maria, adores him as he reminds her of Yanni…he's my husband and her eldest son. She had five boys but I think maybe one or two will be more than enough for us.'

Jade monitored the feed as she listened to the young mother talk about the close-knit Greek family.

After the feed was complete, Jade instilled a tiny amount of sterile water to clear the tubing of residual milk before she capped the tube and settled Costa. Suddenly Soula's voice became unsteady. Jade turned to see the young woman's eyes welling with tears.

'If anything happens to Costa I don't know what I'll do. I love him so much already.' Soula broke down and began sobbing. 'I loved him before he was born.'

Jade closed the incubator door and asked Soula to sit down. It was less than twenty-four hours since she had given birth and she was emotionally and physically drained. Jade gently touched Soula's arm as she spoke. 'Since Costa arrived he has had the best medical care. He might be tiny but he's a strong little boy and putting up a big fight. The injection you were given before delivery has stripped the mucous lining of Costa's lungs enough to allow a head box and avoid a ventilator. He's doing very well.'

'Yes, but Dr Forrester said he's still critical.'

'Soula, every baby here in Neonatal ICU is critical, for different medical reasons. Some are tiny, some have complications but we are all doing our very best to ensure they move to the nursery as soon as they are ready. If Dr Forrester gave you a less than rosy picture, it's because he is being sensibly cautious. It's important that you understand what challenges Costa is facing now and those he will face in coming weeks, and Dr Forrester is telling you everything. That is far better than not knowing what lies ahead.' Jade paused. 'But as he's only just arrived, and after reading Costa's notes, it appears that he is doing very well. We will feed him your milk as soon as it comes in and that will help enormously with his immunity.'

'His father just wants to know that Costa is okay,' she said, mopping her tears. 'I promised Yanni that I'd call as soon as I'd visited this morning. He's up in Roxby in the mines. He works two weeks on and two weeks off and he'd arranged to be here for the birth but Costa arrived eight weeks early. They're trying to arrange a flight down here today for Yanni and he's desperate for any news of his son.' Her words arrived at an increasing speed because of her nerves.

'I can imagine he would be,' Jade told her, empathy in her soft voice. 'It must be such a worry for him, being so far away. As you can probably tell by my accent I'm not from here, so I have no idea where Roxby is located. Is it a big mining town?'

Jade decided to engage Soula in a conversation about the man she clearly adored. It was something tangible and positive and would help the young woman to perhaps focus on something to pull her anxiety down to a manageable level. Jade was fully aware that Soula might within a day or so have to deal with symptoms associated with the postpartum blues, such as mood swings, sleep disturbances and tearfulness, and this would add to her already anxious state. She was glad that Yanni would be arriving soon to support his wife. They would be able to face Costa's hurdles together.

'Roxby is a mining town up north. I've never been there but...' Soula began to slow her words and take breaths. 'When we were trying to get pregnant, Yanni said I should make a trip up there with him because the town has one of the highest birth rates in the whole of Australia.' Soula was trying to appear a little braver than she really felt but her shaky sigh betrayed the anxiety still very close to the surface.

'Really,' Jade replied evenly. 'They might have to bring more televisions into the town if it becomes a problem.'

Soula smiled, a meek smile but still a smile. Happy that the new mother was comfortable, keeping her baby company, Jade headed over to see how her other little patient was progressing. It was time to check his vital signs.

'Looks like you've settled in very well.' The voice like molten chocolate came from close behind her and resonated through every part of her body. 'Even have our new mothers swap tears for smiles. I'm impressed, Nurse Grant.'

Jade tugged at her lower lip with her teeth. She didn't want or need to hear that voice. It was inevitable, she admitted silently, as he was her boss and she had seen him scrubbing in earlier, but it was not welcome. Mitchell Forrester was causing her body and mind to react in ways she had forgotten she had ever felt. She swallowed before she turned to him but it wasn't enough to steady her racing heart when she came face to face with him again. It was ridiculous. Only the day before she had been so angry with him, then had agreed to a truce, and now she found it hard to be near him for very different reasons.

She didn't trust herself.

'I like to see parents smile,' she managed as she struggled to level her rapid breathing. 'But I can't stop to chat, I'm super-busy, just about to check Jasper's vitals. I just finished Costa's feed. His mother is quite anxious but he appears to be doing well. He's feeding, vitals are stable and her husband is expected to arrive soon, which I hope will alleviate her distress to some degree. She needs his support. Oh, and you forgot to tell me last night that we'd be working together. Any reason for that?'

'Thought it might be a pleasant surprise,' he replied with a smile. He wasn't entirely sure why he hadn't told her. Perhaps because he was still trying to figure out in his head how he felt about the working arrangement. And how he felt about her.

Jade couldn't believe how he looked so good even in his scrubs. And how nervous he made her feel and how the words were spilling from her lips at lightning speed. It was as if she were a first-year nursing student suddenly and not the confident neonatal nurse with years of experience under her belt and on her résumé. How she wished he had retained the unkempt look of old. Resistance would have been so easy if he looked like a castaway but now he was causing an awareness of needs and desires she had pushed from her mind for so long. She was not about to join the bevy of nurses at the Eastern Memorial who found his charm irresistible.

'So do we operate any differently from over in the US?' Mitchell asked as he observed her taking baby Johnson's temperature.

Jade reminded herself that if she wanted to keep him at arm's length she had to remain aloof and professional at all times. 'Not that I've noticed. Maybe a few different terms like *obs* when I would say *vitals* but it's not going to be a struggle for me to adapt.'

Mitchell smiled. He thought she would fit in very well. Too well, in fact, he thought as he walked away. He didn't want to become accustomed to having her around.

Jade kept her focus on the baby as she finished recording his vitals and then, satisfied he was progressing well, she closed the incubator door. She was relieved Mitchell was assisting with another small patient that had just arrived in NICU.

The afternoon turned to evening, with Jade liking her temporary new workplace. The other nurses were lovely, a little infatuated with Mitchell but other than that Jade enjoyed working with them. Those who didn't want to sleep with him couldn't praise him enough, and Jade had to agree that he was brilliant with the patients and ensured that the parents felt a part of decision-making around their newborn.

She had overheard his conversations with anxious mothers and fathers during her shift and his bedside manner reduced their unfounded fears and allowed them to understand the real hurdles ahead. He answered their questions honestly but with enough compassion not to add to their heightened anxiety. Jade witnessed his skills as a neonatologist and she knew that she would feel safe if she were a parent and he was the attending doctor diagnosing and arranging a treatment plan for a tiny infant.

The shift came to an end at ten in the evening, and Jade knew that Amber would be tucked into bed and sound asleep. She had called during her late lunch break and spoken to her niece and discovered to her delight that she was enjoying her time splashing in a wading pool. Maureen assured Jade that Amber was wearing sunscreen and inflatable arm bands and that she and Arthur wouldn't take their eyes from her for a second. During the second call, Jade had found out that Amber had dried off from the pool and was busy making cupcakes. It had been a weight off Jade's mind to hear her so happy. She had been safely inside the house and Jade knew that Maureen was very responsible so she had nothing to worry about. Maureen was nothing like her elder son, not likely to run off with Amber on an adventure of any sort.

It was late and dark so Jade was going to get a cab home from the city. She had caught the tram in but, despite the glorious warm evening air, the walk to the tram stop along the dark city road didn't hold much appeal.

'Need a lift?'

Jade knew it was Mitchell without turning her head. Her heart annoyingly skipped a beat and confirmed it. She felt like a teenager the way her body was reacting.

Or overreacting, as she told herself.

'I'm catching a cab, it's a bit late for the tram.'

He walked closer and made Jade very aware of his presence. The cologne on his clothes was faint but still enough to stir her senses.

'I'll give you a lift. I live in the same road, remember, so it's not going out of the way.'

Jade drew a deep breath and in silence she turned around to face the most intense blue eyes. She knew it would be rude to decline his offer but the alarm bells in her head were louder than the ambulance siren as it pulled into the nearby A and E bay.

'You're sure?' she asked, hoping against all hope that in the moments since he'd asked he had suddenly remembered somewhere he had to be on the other side of the city. Or that there was a single young nurse in need of his attention. Anything really that would allow her to squirm her way out of sharing the trip home.

'Very sure,' he insisted. 'I'm in the doctors' car park at the side of the building.'

With reservations and a deep breath, Jade followed her handsome chauffeur into the dimly lit car park. She could see a few cars but had no idea which one belonged to Mitchell. There were a four-wheel-drive, three late-model BMWs, a couple of hatchbacks and a motorbike. She felt pretty sure it was the four-wheel drive as it had roof racks that she assumed would be utilised for his surfboards. The hatchbacks would be a squeeze for his six-foot-two frame, but he might have gone the sophisticated route of the imported sedan.

At this time of the night Jade's concern about her mode of transport was close to zero. She just wanted to get home and put her feet up. And do it without being too close to Mitchell.

'Here,' he said as he held out a motorbike helmet and took her bag from her shoulder. 'This one's for you, and I'll take the bag for safekeeping.'

'You can't be serious.'

'Deadly,' he said, raising one dark eyebrow over a twinkling eye.

Her rising anxiety levels began pumping adrenalin around her tired body. 'I'm honestly not comfortable with the whole bike thing. I think I'll catch a cab.' She felt a tension headache coming on.

'And make me ride home alone?' he asked her with a stare so intense it refused to be ignored. 'Come on, keep me company. It's only a twenty-minute trip.'

Jade felt her heart begin to stampede. But this reaction wasn't purely the fear of the bike. It was the man. If only she hadn't looked at him when he'd looked at her that way. It was almost impossible to remain distant but she had to. She couldn't risk getting close to him. She definitely couldn't let him get under her skin.

'It's not a tough decision,' he said. 'I can assure you that in all the time I've been riding bikes I haven't killed, maimed or lost a single passenger.'

'That's supposed to make me feel better?' Jade asked tartly, taking a step backwards to reclaim some distance between them.

'Come on, lassie, take the boy up on his offer and be off with the pair of you,' said a paediatric consultant Jade recognised from NCIU. Her accent was thick and Jade felt certain it was Irish. She was putting her bag in the back seat of one of the BMW sedans that Jade wished with all of her being was Mitchell's mode of transport. Not for the prestige attached to the vehicle, it was the doors and roof that she wanted. And the console between them.

'You're a wise woman, Maggie O'Donnell, to be sure, to be sure,' Mitchell, said mimicking her accent.

Maggie sharply turned her attention to Mitchell. 'Any more from you, Dr Forrester, and I'll convince the poor girl not to take the ride and I won't be talking to you again, to be sure, to be sure!'

Mitchell smiled as he watched Maggie shake her head

of neat grey curls. 'It's been a long day and I'm in need of a cuppa and some kip so you two can do what you please. I'm away.' With that she reversed from the car park and drove off into the dark, leaving Jade alone with Mitchell again. And a problem.

Why couldn't he just drive a regular car like all the other doctors?

Dread filled her thoughts. It wasn't safe.

For two reasons.

It was a motorbike and they could have an accident. They could be sideswiped, hit a pothole or skid in the rain. It wasn't raining, she admitted to herself, but it still was a bad idea.

And secondly, if she were crazy enough to accept a lift, a bike would force her to wrap her arms around Mitchell just to stop her falling off. There was no way she wanted to be that close to him and feel the warmth of his body close to hers.

'It's a straight run down North Terrace then ANZAC Highway to Glenelg,' he said. As if he read her mind he continued, 'It's not raining, the highway's just been resurfaced so there's no potholes along the way and not much traffic so there's negligible risk of being knocked off the bike.'

'I just don't feel good about it.'

'Have you ever been on a motorbike before?'

Jade nodded reluctantly. She had been on so many motorbike rides that she'd lost count. She'd loved to ride around the winding roads to Malibu on the Pacific Coast Highway. Whether she had been the rider or the passenger, she'd loved the feeling when she'd headed out along the beach road, the faster the better as the fresh ocean breeze had hit her face under the helmet.

'Yes, a few times but—'

'And you're here to tell the tale so that makes two of us. So I say let's get going.'

Jade felt she'd be a hypocrite if she refused and walked back to the cab rank when she knew she had ridden a bike in far more dangerous situations than a quick trip home.

Grudgingly, she accepted the helmet and that simple act elicited a huge smile from Mitchell. He knew that underneath Miss Prim was a woman who wanted to let go and lie naked in the sun. He would just have to take small steps to draw out the real Jade and make her feel comfortable to be herself. He wondered how long she had been hiding beneath the maiden aunt façade. Had it been since Amber was born or something more recent? It would be a challenging few weeks but he would do his best to make Amber's aunt fun to be around for Amber.

It wasn't for him, he told himself. He wanted Jade to lighten up and be fun for her niece, that was all.

He slipped on his helmet, put her bag in the storage compartment of the seat and then climbed on the bike and started the engine.

Jade stood frozen to the spot. Her helmet was securely on her head but her mind was fighting her decision.

Mitchell lifted his visor and reached his hand out to her. His eyes told her a story that she didn't want to hear. He was handsome, intelligent and fun. And she was losing the struggle to refuse his invitation.

She relented and, accepting his hand, climbed on the back of the bike.

His warm scent was all around her, and she prayed that once they hit the road the breeze would make it dissipate, along with the feelings he was stirring in her body. Her hands limply held on to the sides of his body until his strong hands suddenly pulled her hands across his waist in a tighter grip. Her body was pulled against his as they hit the road. Together.

CHAPTER FIVE

'HOME IN ONE PIECE, as promised,' Mitchell announced as he stood holding his helmet beside the shiny black motorbike that had been their carriage home.

Jade was already off the bike and in the driveway, putting distance between them quickly. His proximity during the ride home had been unsettling and now his silhouette against the light of the streetlamp was ridiculously appealing. She had to step away and stay away. If things were different she could see this night having a different ending too. Perhaps a kiss and the promise of another bike ride. But it couldn't end any other way than a polite thank you, she thought as she looked wistfully up at the window where Amber was sleeping.

But she wasn't angry with Mitchell any more. That had subsided. He had his reasons and he was clearly smitten by Amber now. She hoped that their relationship would build over the years and deepen. His dedication to the babies in his care at the hospital and the empathy he had for their parents was clear, and it did raise her opinion of him. His absolute determination to see the tiny children survive against the odds was an admirable quality.

And his gift to Amber of the locket to carry with her

on her adventures all over the world was something that Jade had to admit to herself she would have appreciated a few years ago.

Mitchell was not a bad man but he was still the wrong man for her and she couldn't allow their truce to grow into something more. He was suddenly ticking every box. And some she hadn't known had been there to start with.

It was ironic that it scared Jade how safe she'd felt, taking a risk with Mitchell and riding the motorbike. In the past, she would take risks because she wanted to and because she didn't care about the consequences, but with Mitchell it wasn't like that. She felt protected by him. But she had to remember what was at stake. She had Amber to consider. And they would only be in Adelaide for a few weeks and Mitchell might not even stay that long.

It would be over before it began.

'Thank you for the lift.'

'You're most welcome, and if you need a lift in tomorrow morning I'm happy to oblige.'

Mitchell could see that beneath Jade's sensible exterior was a woman who could let her hair down. Tonight had proved it. She knew how to ride a bike. She'd leaned into the turns, she hadn't been afraid. He hadn't been teaching her anything that she hadn't already known and he liked that about her.

She was fun and adventurous but she was playing a safe hand of cards. He liked to shuffle the deck and take his chances and he suspected that once upon a time she had too. He just had to find that woman inside and draw her out so she didn't raise Amber to be scared of her own shadow.

'Thanks, but I'll be fine to tram it in. I'm on an afternoon shift again tomorrow.'

Perhaps she was more like him than she cared to remember. Independent, happy to have a good time and willing to enjoy what the world had to offer. Only time would tell, he thought as he said goodnight and rode off down the street.

Her head felt light as she entered the house. She'd found the ride exhilarating. Mitchell had been in control of the beast of a bike, and she'd loved that. A little too much, she realised when she quietly climbed into her bed next to Amber's and struggled to fall asleep. The feelings he'd unleashed during the ride had been unexpected. Freedom, fun and…desire. Jade had pushed these feelings to a place from where she'd thought they could never escape. And they hadn't, until now. Until Mitchell had threatened to release all of them at once.

Jade heard Mitchell's motorbike roar past her window next morning and felt her stomach churn and chills run down her spine with the sound. Not ominous chills. Just the opposite. She had been so close to the sound only a few hours before and it had made her feel alive. Now she worried that she could grow to like the feelings he was stirring.

She spent the morning with Amber, playing on the beach, trying desperately to push Mitchell from her mind. He was just a man and she had dated her fair share and ignored even more over the years. Yet the scent of his cologne so close to her and the feeling of her arms around his hard body as they'd ridden together were haunting her waking thoughts. He was making her question her safe life choices.

Maureen decided she would take her granddaughter to the shops on Jetty Road to find a few 'sparkly things' when Jade left for work. Jade wasn't entirely sure what 'sparkly things' meant but Amber was excited by the prospect so Jade was happy as she headed off for her second shift at the hospital.

Her shift began at two. There was handover and she was informed of a new airlifted baby from Melbourne who would be in her care. She hadn't been named yet so they referred to her as Baby Morey.

'There was no alternative, considering they were short of incubators in Melbourne. The hospitals over there had a whole run of prem deliveries within a few days. They're grateful the Eastern Memorial could accept her,' Mandy told Jade as they neared the incubator. 'She's tiny but a fighter.'

'Why didn't the parents travel with the infant?'

'The mother delivered her via Caesarean after a car accident,' Mandy told Jade as they neared the incubator. 'I saw the report that arrived. Four-car pile-up on the Tullamarine Freeway near the airport.'

'Are the parents all right? Did they survive?' Jade's voice suddenly became shaky as her hands hovered nervously. She prayed they were both alive, she didn't want to hear anything else. *Déjà vu* instantly made her skin crawl and her stomach knot.

'They're both stable and off the critical list. Her mother has a hairline fracture of her collarbone, a punctured lung and, of course, the postnatal effects of the Caesarean birth, and Cara's father has damage to his vertebrae and a fractured hip. He's in Spinal Injuries.'

Jade swallowed hard. The infant they were attending had entered the world the same way Amber had three years previously. The time peeled away in an instant as she looked at the baby lying innocently in the incubator, completely unaware of what had happened, all the while holding tenuously to her own life. But she did still have her parents. However injured they were, they would pull through and be a part of her life. Jade was happy for the little girl.

Mandy left Jade as she needed to tend to another tiny patient. NICU was at capacity, with all of the nursing staff, including Mandy, rushed off their feet. Jade was grateful the other nurse hadn't had time to notice the tears welling in her eyes. Amber's fight to stay alive and the battle her parents had lost hit home at lightning speed and brought emotions rushing to the surface.

'The paediatrician had noted suspected respiratory distress, causing cyanosis, but I wasn't convinced and I ran some additional tests,' Mitchell told a small group of medical students as he approached the new arrival and Jade. 'The bluish discoloration of the skin and nail beds would indicate respiratory distress but the degree of cyanosis was not proportional to what was shown in the X-rays that accompanied the baby from Melbourne. And it has not been decreasing with increased inspired oxygen and the tests quickly confirmed congestive heart failure.'

He then turned his attention to Jade. 'Nurse Grant, can you move Baby Morey to a radiant heat warmer within the next fifteen minutes so we can maintain her body temperature?'

'Certainly,' Jade replied, trying to blink away the tears before they ran down her cheeks and anyone noticed them.

But Mitchell did. He noticed everything about Jade,

even though he didn't want to. He decided to release the students, who had been with him for most of the morning and were due to end their time in NICU. They looked exhausted and no doubt had information overload, which he suggested might be abated by a coffee in the cafeteria.

As the students left, he called another nurse to take over. 'I need to speak with Nurse Grant for a moment but in her absence I want both cardiorespiratory and oxygen saturation monitoring and I'm prescribing digoxin. Dosages are in the notes and I want close observation until Nurse Grant returns.'

Jade had turned to walk away. She didn't want to be confronted about her reaction. She didn't want or need his concern.

'Nurse Grant, please come with me for a moment.' He kept his professional tone in front of the others then gently took her arm and directed her to a small office nearby used by consultants and residents when they needed to speak with parents in private. He closed the door and turned to her.

'Jade, what's wrong?' he asked, releasing her from his firm hold but not the intensity of his gaze.

'Nothing,' she lied, and blinked even harder as she tried to look anywhere but at Mitchell. 'I'm fine.'

'You're anything but fine.'

'I'll be okay. I don't want special treatment.' She looked up, and his expression wasn't what she had been expecting. It wasn't judgmental. It was empathetic and real and etched into every part of his face. And it suddenly and unexpectedly allowed her to give in to her feelings. Tears that had built up for so long began streaming down her face.

She hadn't cried since the funeral. Her feelings had been bottled up inside. She had been strong because she'd felt she'd had no other choice. There was no one for her to lean on while she was Amber's only support.

'You're so far from okay.' Without hesitation, he reached out, put his arm around her and pulled her into his arms, and she didn't pull away.

'Is it Amber?' He murmured the question as he gently stroked her hair. 'Are you worried about her?'

Jade knew as the moments passed that, as much as it felt good to have a man's arms around her, she couldn't stay there for ever. And particularly not in Mitchell's arms. He wouldn't be there for ever; neither would she. It was crazy to let him into her heart. She slowly moved from his embrace and a place that had made her feel safe, if only for a moment.

'Amber's fine, honestly, Mitchell…' She hesitated for a minute to gather her thoughts and put any growing feelings for him away. 'It was the new arrival in NICU. The baby was delivered by C-section after a motor vehicle accident…and it just brought everything back. I have to toughen up. I'm working on it.'

Mitchell didn't want Jade to toughen up at all. She didn't need additional walls. He wanted more than anything to break down the ones she had. She might not be his usual fun-loving, easygoing type but suddenly he wondered if just a casual good time was enough any more. Being around Jade for the past few days, even putting Amber to bed and all it entailed, had not been the chore he had imagined. He had enjoyed every minute of that special time with his niece and with Jade.

His type was fast becoming a cute Californian girl with a pixie cut and the dress sense of someone's maiden aunt but the soul and depth of no one he had ever met before.

'The best nurses are those with empathy and compassion,' he told her as she turned to face him. 'You have both. Don't hide what is inside you.'

Jade didn't want to meet his gaze. She wanted to pull herself together and face the job outside. 'I need to get back to work. We're short enough on staff, let alone with me sitting in here, snivelling. I'm being self-indulgent and silly.'

'You're not being either, so take a minute,' he continued. 'And when you're ready, head back out. If you prefer, I will switch your patient roster.'

Jade took a deep breath and gently shook her head. 'I want to stay with my patient. I really do.'

'It's your call, if you're up to it.'

'I am,' she said, crossing to the door, feeling the need to put space between them. He was much too appealing on a whole other level now. It wouldn't just be his smouldering looks that would make it difficult. Now that Jade knew he had a heart, and a level of compassion and empathy she hadn't thought he possessed, it would make it that much more difficult to be around him. But that wasn't his problem. It was hers.

Jade walked back into NCIU and straight to her patient. Mitchell followed behind her. He admired her dedication and compassion, and although he wished she had taken some time out, he respected her wishes and acted accordingly.

'I noticed her slow feeding time so I want you to switch to gavage feeding so she's not working hard for the food and can conserve energy. Later we'll try her sucking again but provide higher caloric formula. And I'll see if they've decided on a name yet. I don't want to refer to her by her surname. She needs her own name.'

Mitchell's last few words made her smile. He genuinely cared so much for these babies and it wasn't just his clinical abilities that impressed Jade. He treated the babies as little people with feelings, extending even to having a proper name. She was falling for the man, and there was no way to stop her tumble.

Jade followed Mitchell's instructions, inserted a gavage tube into the tiny stomach and began the slow feed. Aware of the management of babies with congestive heart failure, Jade placed her in a semi-erect position for feeding and burped her every half an ounce to minimise the chance of vomiting after the feed. Jade felt an extra-special bond with this baby, who had a small tuft of blonde hair on her crown. Jade planned on spending additional time with Baby Morey as she didn't have a mother who could visit and she wanted to provide that additional care.

Mitchell returned briefly to give additional instructions regarding the baby's management and feeding but noticed Jade was already implementing those procedures. He was impressed with her abilities and initiative so did not interrupt. He just wanted to share something with her.

'Baby Morey's name is Alina. It apparently means light,' he told her.

Jade lifted her eyes to meet his smile. A rush of warmth flowed over her. Mitchell was so pleased the baby had a name. It seemed to mean something to him. Jade could tell his happiness at bestowing the name on the baby was genuine. He was genuine. He was a good man. And it scared her that she was starting to *only* see the good in him.

Quickly, she averted her eyes and returned her focus to Alina.

He might be a good man but she needed to remind herself that she wasn't looking for a man, good or not. But it was a message that was becoming less audible every minute.

'Another delivery,' Alli announced as she wheeled in another tiny patient and transferred the baby to a radiant heat warmer near Jade. 'This is Liam. Dad's just scrubbing in, Mum's still in Recovery. Caesarean delivery, gestational age twenty-nine weeks.'

A few minutes later a very worried-looking man in his late forties arrived. He was still wearing his blue disposable scrubs from Theatre.

'Over here, Mr Phillips,' Alli called. 'Dr Forrester is on his way. Just take a seat beside your son.'

'Oh, my God, he's so small,' the man said anxiously as he looked at the baby lying on a radiant heat warmer. He looked around at the other babies and then back at his own. Jade could see the concern on his face. He was a big man but his fear was almost palpable.

'Mr Phillips,' Mitchell said as he approached the newborn, 'I'm Mitchell Forrester and I'll be assessing your son.'

Nervously, the man asked, 'Why isn't he inside one of those?' He was pointing to an incubator. 'Don't you have enough of them? Wouldn't that keep him warmer? Shouldn't he at least have a blanket on him?'

'There are different levels of care available in Neonatal and it depends on your baby's needs where he will be placed,' Mitchell began to explain. 'At the moment we need to access Liam, he will need complex care and the incubator limits access for the medical staff. Please don't worry, your son is being kept warm and is in the best place for him at this time.'

'Okay, if you're sure.'

'I am, Mr Phillips.'

The man looked around to see other parents sitting beside their babies so tentatively he sat and began unconsciously wringing his hands. 'How long will he need to stay here in Intensive Care?'

'I can't give you an accurate idea yet. Premature babies need additional help while their bodies catch up on the growth and development they missed in the womb. He'll need assistance to stay warm because he can't control his own body temperature yet. And Liam is just over two pounds, so he's still too immature to feed. He'll need a tube that carries milk into his stomach,' Mitchell told him as he warmed the stethoscope and gently placed it on Liam's tiny chest.'

'But my wife wants to breastfeed. She told me that.'

'She can express milk until Liam's strong enough to feed but we need to get his weight up and feeding is tiring so we need to make it easier for him,' Jade added, aware that Mitchell was listening to Liam's heart.

The man understood and remained silent until Mitchell removed the stethoscope and put it back around his neck.

'How many staff do you have here to take care of the babies?' he asked. 'Will there be enough to look after Liam if more babies arrive?'

'Yes, there are more than enough staff to cover the patients and any unexpected arrivals such as Liam. You will see many different staff providing care to your son over the coming weeks. Neonatal Intensive Care has a number of special nurses like Alli who you just met, and we are very fortunate to have Jade, who is over from the States, bringing her knowledge and expertise from a large teaching hospital is Los Angeles.'

Mitchell spoke with pride about Jade and it wasn't lost on her.

'Then there's Laura, the senior nurse in charge of the unit,' he continued. 'And the neonatologist, who, in Liam's case, is me. I'll be leading your baby's care. On top of that there are other specialist doctors, such as surgeons if the need arises, and physiotherapists to help with your baby's development, radiographers and dieticians, and then there are social workers to help you with family issues and support that might be needed after you take your baby home in a few months' time. There is quite literally a small intensive care army to provide everything that your family will need over the coming weeks and months.'

Jade was still listening as Mitchell handled the barrage of questions with ease. He related so well and wasn't short with his answers. He took his time to quell the man's heightened anxiety and let him catch his breath. And the way he had spoken about her made her feel valued and important and it resonated in her heart.

'It's important that you visit as much as possible and no matter how many staff are attending to Liam, remember first and foremost he needs you and your wife. Having a parent here as much as possible makes such a difference to the child.'

Jade saw the man relax his shoulders into the chair. He had arrived feeling out of his depth and overwhelmed, but Mitchell had given him a sense of purpose and validated his questions.

'I'm just going to continue my examination and you are most welcome to stay, or if you would like to check on your wife and let her know Liam is safe with us, you could come back down together. I'll be here all afternoon and can answer any other questions you have. And there will be new questions every day so don't hesitate to ask anything you're concerned about. This neonatal unit has an open-door policy so parents can visit twenty-four hours a day.'

'I think I might go and see my wife then and let her know everything's under control,' he said, climbing to his feet. 'But if anything changes and you want me back here, call my wife's ward and I'll be straight back down.'

'We'll be sure to let you know, but Liam is stable at the moment. So you come back down when you're both ready.'

Jade watched the man shuffle out of the unit in somewhat of a daze. There was so much to take in and he was clearly also concerned about his wife. They had a long road ahead of them until their son was in the nursery and preparing to go home.

'Have you had dinner yet?' Mitchell asked Jade as she was leaving NICU for her tea break.

'Heading there now. I have an hour, so I intend to put my feet up and grab a wrap or a salad in the cafeteria.'

'I've got a better idea,' Mitchell said as the elevator doors opened and they both stepped inside. 'A little Italian restaurant across the road. They serve the best pasta and they do it quickly. They know we don't have much time. It's delicious and just like being in Italy.'

Jade was surprised by the invitation but it happened so quickly she didn't have time to refuse. Or think it through. Perhaps that was a good thing, she surmised as they stood at the traffic lights a minute later, waiting to cross the main road as darkness was falling.

'I should have asked if you like Italian food,' he said after a minute or two. 'I guess I just assumed everyone does.'

'You guessed right with me, I love Italian.'

The meal came out quickly and they were halfway to finishing their risottos when Mitchell decided to tell her about the pool and what he'd seen. He had been thinking it over since it had happened and had decided that he wanted and needed to be honest with Jade. He had no intention of embarrassing her but he felt she had the right to know.

He just wasn't entirely sure how to raise it.

'You seem quiet suddenly,' Jade commented as she pushed the risotto around with her fork. She was borderline full but searching for more of the tasty grilled chicken pieces. The herbs were amazing and Mitchell was right, the food was great.

'There was something I wanted to tell you,' Mitchell began, and then hesitated. He wasn't sure how Jade would react but he hoped she might see the humorous side of it. He had definitely not taken advantage of the situation by looking back at her after the initial shock sighting.

'Go on,' she urged as she gave up on trying to fit in any more food and just sipped on her iced water.

Mitchell took a nervous sip of his own water. 'The other morning, I came to the house to assemble the sound system. Arthur had no clue how to put it together so he asked me to do it.'

Jade had no idea where the conversation was heading and why Mitchell thought there was a need to tell her about his handyman work. 'Was this when you served me breakfast in bed with Amber?'

'Yes.'

'So did you get it done before I woke up?'

He drew a deep breath and continued. 'No, it was later in the morning.'

'But I was home all morning after Maureen and Arthur took Amber out, and I didn't see you,' she returned with a puzzled look.

'No, you didn't see me, but I saw you sun-baking by the pool.'

Embarrassment hit and Jade put her hand to her mouth and closed her eyes for a moment. 'I thought there was no one home or I would never have gone out in the sun like that.'

'I just wanted to say that I looked away as soon as I realised what you were doing. Your secret's safe with me but I wanted us to have a level of honesty. I didn't want to keep it from you.'

'What I was doing? What are you talking about? I was sun-baking…that's all. You hardly had to avert your eyes, I'm sure you've seen it a million times before.'

Mitchell stared at Jade with a puzzled look. She was so casual about sunbathing naked and it took him by surprise.

'Hardly a million,' he remarked.

'There were so many bikinis on the beach the other day.'

'Yes, there were, but you chose not to wear one and… and that's okay…'

'What on earth are you talking about?' she cut in abruptly. Her eyes were wide and completed her horrified expression. 'I was wearing a bikini.'

'Not by the time I got there,' he told her. 'I walked to the shed to get some tools and when I closed the door I saw you lying there on the sun lounge with nothing on. I dropped the tools, picked them up and left.'

Jade sat up in her chair and wiped the corners of her mouth with the white napkin. 'I don't know whose house you were in, but it couldn't have been the same one as me because I had on a string bikini. I have to admit it isn't something I would parade around Amber but it's all I had and I wanted to enjoy the sun. Clearly, you don't know me very well to think for a moment I sunbathe in the nude.' Jade dropped her voice to barely a whisper. 'It's not what I'd do.'

Jade thought back to her wildest days and even then she would have drawn the line at that.

'Jade, we've only known each other for three days, so I can't say I really know much about you at all. What I do know is that you're a brilliant nurse, amazing with both the parents and the neonates, and you've done an amazing job of bringing up Amber. She's a sweetheart and she adores and depends on you. I'm not about to judge you for skinny-dipping. In fact, quite the opposite,' he said with a twinkle in his eye.

'In your parents' pool…that would be so wrong.'

'My family owes you so much for how you have raised Amber and been there for her every step of the way. Honestly, Jade, after what you've done for our family you can pretty much do anything you want and get away with it.'

'You can stop right there. It's been hard at times but she is a joy and so precious and I couldn't imagine a day without her,' Jade told him. 'But no matter how *grateful* your family might be, I wouldn't overstep the mark and skinny-dip in their pool…ever. Stripping down to a bikini is a stretch for me, let alone running around the pool naked.'

Mitchell smiled but wasn't sure why she wouldn't wear a bikini around Amber. It was Australia and the twenty-first century so there was no reason that she couldn't, and from what he had seen there was absolutely no reason for her not to wear one. Maybe she was telling the truth. Maybe she had been wearing a swimsuit and his eyes had misled him.

'What colour is your bikini?'

'It's kind of skin-coloured Lycra. You could call it nude. Maybe you should check your distance vision.'

'Damn, maybe I should,' Mitchell said, laughing. 'If only I'd known that you were wearing a swimsuit, I would've stopped and focused. But, Jade, I must say from my brief glance you looked stunning.'

Jade felt her cheeks redden with the compliment. She knew Mitchell really had looked away quickly. He was a gentleman. If he had stopped to look at her he would have quickly seen she'd been wearing a bikini so decency really had made him look the other way in a hurry.

Although now she felt quite self-conscious that he had seen her in the skimpy swimsuit and she felt the need to explain why she had been wearing something so at odds with her normal dress code.

'I haven't worn it in years. I don't think it's the right image any more, particularly around a little girl. I think Amber would prefer to see me in something a bit more respectable.'

Mitchell did not break eye contact as he looked at

his dinner companion and the woman who was slowly claiming more than his attention. She was getting closer each day to claiming his heart. 'I would have to disagree with you on that one, Jade. I'm sure Amber would think her aunty looked gorgeous in a bikini. I know I did.'

CHAPTER SIX

THE CALL CAME through from the Royal Flying Doctor Service just as Jade was scrubbing in the next afternoon. It was her last shift for the week, then she would have four days off with Amber to visit the zoo and have a birthday picnic.

'I can leave immediately,' Mitchell said as he saw the paediatric consultant scrubbing in. He knew NICU would be well covered. 'Do you have the gestational age?'

'Around thirty-four weeks.'

'Thirty-four weeks, so not critical, but there are two babies to consider. If you have your flight nurse ready I'll bring a neonatal nurse with midwifery experience.' Mitchell knew exactly whom he would take on the trip. He had spied her scrubbing in for her shift.

'We can transport the three of you.'

'Good, as I said, thirty-four weeks is not critical but twins can mean smaller babies so if there are complications I would prefer to have additional hands on board. Please let the pilot know I will arrange ambulance transportation to the airport straight away. ETA fifteen minutes.'

Mitchell hung up the phone and, looking around the NICU, quickly found Jade. With long, purposeful strides he crossed to her just as she was about to take Costa's obs.

'I need you to come with me. It's urgent.' He signalled Alli to come and take over Costa's care from Jade.

Jade didn't doubt for a second by the tone of Mitchell's voice and the look on his face that it was something serious. His brow was knitted and his jaw rigid as he spoke.

'I need you to walk as we talk,' he said, leading her from NICU. 'I want you to travel with me to the Outback, to near a small town in the central Flinders Ranges. It's called Blinman and it's about an hour's flight from here. We have premature labour with twins and the town has no medical facilities. The woman was on a camping retreat with her husband and friends when her waters broke.'

'Why me?'

'Because you have both neonatal and midwifery skills and you have just scrubbed in, so you are fresh,' he replied matter-of-factly. 'Alli and Laura have some midwifery behind them but they are about an hour from finishing long shifts. They're tired and you're better placed to help.'

They had reached the doors of the hospital and the ambulance bay at a ridiculously fast pace.

'But what about Amber?'

'She won't even know you've gone with me. It will be just over an hour's flight time and by the sound of it the babies are close to being born so we will be back by dinner at the latest and I'll let you knock off and go home the moment we get back. You're not due to finish until late so you'll be home earlier than usual.'

'Isn't there a flight nurse and doctor on board already?'

'No, just a flight nurse. She will meet us at the airport. This is still deemed a high-risk delivery and there is enough room in the emergency retrieval aircraft for a three-person medical team, the mother and two portable cribs According to the RFDS, the mother is not fully dilated but well on the way so I'm thinking maybe four hours all up. Your shift has only just begun so we should return in plenty of time for you to get home to kiss Amber goodnight. I'll text home and let them know we're both in the air and we'll be back in a few hours.'

'Why would an expectant mother head to the bush? What was out in the middle of nowhere?' Jade asked as she and Mitchell climbed into the ambulance.

'Sounds like eastern suburbs hippies, doing yoga and meditation for a week,' he returned with a roll of his eyes. 'Eastern suburbs means nothing to you, I know, but basically they are well educated, financially secure people who head to the bush to centre themselves once or twice a year. I have nothing against it but travelling over rough terrain probably wasn't the best idea. It may or may not have brought about the early labour but it's happened and she's in trouble. Last antenatal check, twin two was still breech.'

'She's definitely going to need our help, then,' Jade replied.

They arrived at the plane fifteen minutes later. The pilot warned them of bad weather rolling in from a tropical storm in the northeast, bringing a high chance of turbulence. He had exchanged intermittent radio contact with the patient's partner, Jeremy, on the ground as his mobile service coverage wasn't great and the storm-clouds were interfering. He would be making his way to the nearest makeshift airstrip. The flight nurse had ascertained that the woman was coping with the pain, she was as comfortable as could be expected in a tent and had another female companion with her. Then radio contact had been lost.

'Emma Kingston,' the flight nurse introduced herself as she boarded and buckled up.

'Mitchell Forrester, neonatologist, Eastern Memorial.'

'Jade Grant, neonatal nurse.'

'And midwife,' Mitchell added, with a sense of pride for the woman sitting beside him.

'Good to have you both on board,' Emma said as she looked over the notes that had been sent to her phone and handed them to Jade and Mitchell to read. 'Twins, one breech, in a bush delivery will be challenging.'

'What are the biggest risks in your opinion?' Mitchell asked Jade as they became airborne.

'I have concerns with the safety of natural breech delivery and we obviously can't perform a C-section. Natural birth requires at least the first foetus to be cephalic, which I'm noting here was the case at the last antenatal visit, but if the first baby is anything but this then a natural delivery is unsafe.'

'The RFDS operator said her obstetrician is confident that hasn't changed,' Mitchell told her.

'Then we just have the normal issues after the first infant is delivered. With the cervix still wide open, the umbilical cord can make its way down and this can be dangerous for the remaining foetus. Then there's the risk that if the uterus shrinks rapidly with the delivery of the first twin, then the placenta can separate. As I said before, there's always a small risk with twin delivery of the need for a C-section for the second twin, and we won't have that option in the bush.'

Mitchell considered Jade's concerns for a moment. 'Then let's hope for everyone's sake that the birth is straightforward as I want both babies out ASAP.'

Emma nodded her reply. She had been a flight nurse for over fifteen years with the RFDS but twins in remote areas was a worry. Not wanting to overthink the situation, she slipped on her headphones, pulled out some reports and began reading and making revisions.

The increasing cloud cover made it a bumpy flight and a little nerve-racking for Jade. Each pocket of air that lifted and dropped the small plane sent Jade's stomach into a tailspin. Her heart was beating at an alarming rate but she did her best to mask her concern.

'Are you okay?' Mitchell asked when he heard the sudden intake of air by Jade. 'I thought this would be a piece of cake compared to the long-haul.'

'Not a huge lover of small aircraft,' she said, still trying to control her emotions.

Emma was engaged in her paperwork and didn't seem perturbed by it at all. But there was more to it for Jade. She really didn't want to discuss her recently acquired fear of nearly everything with a man who had daredevil on his résumé. He would never understand her love of thrills had flown out the window when Amber had arrived. She wasn't scared for her own sake. It was the thought of Amber losing another person from her life that scared Jade to the core. No one deserved to experience loss the way Amber had without even being aware

yet of what had been taken. One day she would understand more fully and Jade wanted to be there in one piece
to help her though that realisation.

'We'll be fine. This weather might seem frighten-
ing to you but not to the pilot, who will be very experienced,' his deep but still silky-smooth voice reassured
her. Mitchell looked at Jade and realised that what he had
deemed slight turbulence was really unnerving her. His
bedside manner kicked in and he changed the subject.
'How about you tell me why you chose the noble profes-
sion of neonatal nursing and midwifery and then I will
bore you with why I became a neonatologist.'

Jade considered the very handsome passenger beside
her and she appreciated he was trying to distract her.
She felt she knew him better now after they'd worked
together for two days and, of course, the enlightening
lunch. It concerned her more that she was increasingly
finding him as attractive on the inside as on the outside.

Without warning, the plane dropped, and Mitchell
instinctively reached his hand across to Jade's and held
it tightly.

She didn't pull away. His skin was so warm. His grip
so firm. It wasn't the turbulence that took her breath. She
swallowed and tried not to look down to her lap, where
his hand was protectively covering hers. His touch was
unsettling but she had to admit silently, although it was
ridiculous, that she suddenly felt better. Again. This was
the second time that Mitchell had made her fears disappear with his touch. It was silly to think that his hand
on hers could protect her in an emergency landing. But
it felt as if it could. It also felt wonderful to have someone want to reassure her. And hold her.

Jade knew what she had to do. And it was very different from what she wanted to do. She wanted to let him protect her for a few minutes longer. She wanted to relish that feeling of his skin against hers. But she needed to pull away and take care of herself. She had been doing it alone and there was no reason to change that now. She couldn't rely on Mitchell. She couldn't let him in.

'I fell into it literally,' she said, pulling her hand free to supposedly check the time on her wristwatch. 'I was fourteen and I'd been skateboarding and took a tumble down some steps. I was attempting a stupid manoeuvre that didn't pan out and I was admitted to A and E for a broken wrist. Before that I had no idea what I wanted to do but, watching the nurses, I decided that was my career path.'

'So why neo and midwifery after an A and E admission?' he asked, aware that she had strategically withdrawn her hand and set the purely professional boundaries yet again. He wasn't about to push that boundary.

'On student placement I felt at home both in NICU and Obstetrics. I trained to be a midwife but also wanted to work in Neonatal so undertook additional training so I could work across both. What about you?'

'I left school and backpacked around Australia and then headed to Asia and Africa,' he returned quickly, not wanting a lull in conversation that would let Jade think about the size of the plane and the worsening weather outside. 'I saw what was needed in the developing countries that I visited and decided that I needed to qualify to be of any use so I headed home, applied to study medicine at Adelaide Uni and then specialised. It was a long haul but worth it. Once I was qualified and had completed my residency I returned to Africa and signed on with Médecins Sans Frontières. I worked in small villages and two refugee camps. They had squat when it came to medical equipment, but as a team we did save lives and improve the quality of those who may have been handicapped without early intervention.'

Jade had had no idea that he had been providing life-saving medical assistance to people who would otherwise be denied access to even the most basic health care. Suddenly she realised that the man she had judged as irresponsible was, in fact, quite the opposite. He didn't want ties but he certainly wanted to give to those who needed him most. Mitchell was quite complicated and not a man just after a good time.

'But now you're home,' she said, not really sure why she did and even less sure of why she kept going with that line of questioning. 'Will you stay here or head back overseas?' It was none of her business and she wasn't sure why she wanted to know.

Mitchell paused to think. He hadn't made plans, he never really had after his initial decision to study medicine. Everything else had just seemed to happen. He'd gone where opportunities and challenges arose and where he could avoid commitment. Mitchell had lived his adult life with a 'fly by the seat of his pants' attitude to life and he liked it that way.

'I heard that there was an opening they couldn't fill in NICU at the Eastern and thought it would be a good chance to catch up with family. Haven't really thought about how long or what my plan is, I'll just take it as it comes.'

The plane entered heavy grey clouds and rocked from side to side a little.

'I'm afraid the storm front arrived a little early,' the

pilot announced. 'Might get a little rough but shouldn't be too long before we're through to the other side.'

Jade felt her breathing stall as the plane lurched and jolted. She swallowed anxiously but very quickly the plane steadied and so did her breathing. She looked nervously from the window at the solid wall of grey and white fluff surrounding the small plane. She had to be brave, and with Mitchell so close she found it a little easier. It was only slight turbulence and perhaps the worst was already over.

Suddenly the plane dropped about fifty feet from its flight path. Steadiness disappeared as Jade felt her stomach churn and her heart begin to pound. She gripped the armrests, her knuckles quickly turning white. Without thinking, Mitchell's arms held her tightly. He didn't care that she had tried to build a barrier. He ignored what she wanted and gave her what he knew at that moment she needed. Security and a sense that everything would be okay.

Mitchell had travelled in enough light aircraft over the years to know they would be fine but she didn't have that experience. He understood her fear was very real and he didn't hesitate to reach out to her.

Jade didn't pull away, even after the turbulence subsided. She felt like she had found her safe harbour with Mitchell. And this time she wasn't about to tell it any other way, to him or to herself. It was the truth. He made her sense of fear lessen and it was as if she could halve the worry, knowing he was there to lean on. She could not remember the last time she'd felt that she could rely on someone, more particularly a man. She had never let herself feel that way.

As she looked down at the strong hand that was

covering hers so warmly and the arm that was holding her tight, she wondered if Maureen and Arthur had raised *two* exceptional sons.

CHAPTER SEVEN

THE PLANE LANDED without incident and the medical team quickly unloaded their kits, including two portable incubators, and made their way to the woman's partner, who had been waiting at the makeshift runway with his four-wheel-drive.

'I'm so bloody relieved to see you,' he began as he helped to load the equipment into the back of the vehicle. 'I left Sophie's best friend, Wendy, with her. She's had four kids of her own so I figured she would be more use than me,' he told them as they climbed into the vehicle. 'It's only a ten-minute drive from here but I can get Wendy on the phone for you if you like. My hand-free connection's not good so I'll call before I start out and give you the phone.'

Jade watched as he pulled up the number. His fingers were shaking and beads of perspiration were covering his brow. The sun was warm and the air was dry. It was clearly nerves causing his reaction.

'I have the doctors with me,' he said into the mobile phone then put it on loudspeaker and handed it over.

'Hi, Wendy, this is Jade Grant, I'm a midwife from the Eastern Memorial Hospital and I have with me Mitchell Forrester, a neonatal specialist, and also Emma, the

Royal Flying Doctor Service flight nurse. The plan is for us to be there to deliver the twins and we are a little under ten minutes away. How far apart are Sophie's contractions?'

'About three minutes. I really hope you make it here. I've had four of my own but not in a tent and I had an epidural with all of them so Sophie's doing it the hard way. She's on a clean sleeping bag on all fours to help with the pain because I don't have any painkillers to give her.'

'Three minutes should give us time. I'm happy to hear she's in a clean and dry environment. Can you see the head of a baby yet?'

'Yes. The top of the first twin's head is crowning and Sophie's got the urge to bear down but I've told her to try to hold off until you get here, which I know is easy for me to say.'

'I'm glad she can see a head,' Mitchell said. 'At least the first is not breech and maybe there's a chance the second has turned in utero.'

Jade nodded her agreement with Mitchell's comment and turned her attention back to the surrogate midwife. 'We are only a few minutes away now, Wendy, and you are doing a great job. Just keep Sophie calm, discourage her from pushing, and if you can massage her back it might help with the pain.'

Jade kept talking to Wendy as the four-wheel-drive manoeuvred through the rough terrain to the campsite. It was obvious to them all why the man had not attempted to take his wife into town once labour had started. Jade was surprised, with the way they were all thrown about, that labour hadn't started when the campers had first arrived. It was not the ideal place for an expectant mother to holiday only six weeks from delivery of twins but clearly by the number of tents she could see at the site, this was a majority choice holiday destination.

As they pulled up Mitchell, Jade and Emma hurriedly climbed out with their equipment. Quite a few people had gathered outside the tent that had become the make-shift birthing suite. They were all trying to offer advice and although it was heartfelt, Jade knew that it probably wasn't helping Sophie or Wendy.

'Please make way.' Mitchell's voice was firm and the small crowd parted as the medical team approached. Someone held open the tent entrance for them. They had arrived just in time. Sophie was already pushing. Jade covered her hands generously in antibacterial solution, slipped on some gloves and pulled the cord clamps from the birthing kit, along with the Syntocinon to assist with the afterbirth. She dropped to her knees for the delivery.

'Do you want me on my back?' Sophie managed to ask before the pain took her breath away.

'No, you're in a good position on all fours. It opens the pelvis right up, rather than being on your back. You're doing a wonderful job, Sophie,' Jade told her in a soft, calm voice. 'Just keeping breathing slowly…'

Jade's words were cut short by the next painful con-traction.

'Can you dampen the towel on her forehead a little?' Jade directed Jeremy. 'It's warm in here and it might help.'

Jeremy dipped the towel in a basin of water that had been brought to the makeshift birthing suite earlier and began gently mopping his wife's brow. 'I'm so sorry, darling, that I asked you to come here. It was a stupid idea but I thought you had another six weeks or more.'

'I'm not sorry we came on the camping trip,' she

muttered, between panting and pushing. 'But with this god-awful pain, I'm just sorry that I ever had sex with you. And, for the record, I'm never doing it again!'

Another powerful contraction came and the first baby's head emerged. A mass of black hair first, then a wrinkled forehead and tiny face.

'Just push slowly as you breathe,' Jade told her. 'We don't want to rush the baby.'

There were a few more contractions and Sophie's first baby was born into Jade's waiting hands. 'You have a little girl.'

Mitchell stepped closer and with sterile hands he reached for the tiny girl, who was not as small as he had imagined she would be for the gestational age. Given their surroundings, he was glad there must have been a discrepancy in dates, as a low birth weight baby might have struggled with a natural birth. Jade clamped and cut the cord quickly, and Mitchell wrapped her in sterile sheeting and took her aside to check her. Emma could not put the child to the mother's breast, as there was the second baby to deliver.

Another contraction began and the second baby was on its way quickly. A foot appeared and then with the next contraction it disappeared again inside Sophie.

'It appears that that we are looking at a breech birth after all,' Jade announced as Emma watched on, ready to collect the second baby so that Jade could look after Sophie during the third stage of delivery. 'I prefer "hands-off" breech births if possible so we will be taking this slowly.'

The next painful contraction came, and Sophie groaned loudly.

Both feet appeared this time and then with each

following contraction a little more of the second baby was exposed. With each breath Sophie pushed her second baby a little farther into the world. With concern on his face, her husband mopped her forehead as Jade coached her through the process. A little while later, with no intervention, the hips and stomach of the equally good-sized second baby girl emerged. Finally her little face and then her mop of thick black hair appeared.

'Another girl,' Jade announced.

Mitchell watched and saw that while her little heart was beating and the cord was still pulsing, she was not breathing on her own. He carefully handed the first baby to Emma, then placed an infant non-rebreather over the baby's nose and mouth and began resuscitation. He had been prepared as it was commonplace for breech babies.

'Breathe, baby girl,' Jeremy called to his tiny newborn daughter.

Jade could see the panic on his face and Sophie's. 'Don't worry,' she reassured them. 'It's not unusual and Dr Forrester knows exactly what to do.'

A few moments later the little girl began crying and so was Jeremy with joy and relief. Jade gave Sophie the prepared shot and the placentas arrived with a single contraction for each. Jade checked the placentas thoroughly to ensure they were complete and nothing had been retained in Sophie's uterus that could lead to haemorrhage, as she was already at increased risk of haemorrhage from delivering twins. Jade tended to Sophie as Mitchell and Emma tended to the two baby girls. Mitchell checked the second baby's vital signs and, like her twin, she was in good health with a good weight.

'You've been fortunate. Even with a breech birth you

won't be requiring any stitches,' Jade announced after the birth.

Mitchell had assessed both babies and noted that although they were small they were healthy and would need no additional support. Clearly there had been some mix-up with dates and for all concerned it was a welcome mistake.

'Although I have no concerns about the health of your daughters, we need to get mother and babies to hospital immediately,' Mitchell announced, as he gave the first-born to the father for a cuddle while he packed away his medical kit. 'Can you drive us back to the airstrip? I will need you to take it very slowly.'

Jeremy looked with joy at the tiny miracle in his arms, then at his second daughter, being held by Emma. He turned to look lovingly at his wife as a smile played at the corners of his mouth. 'They are perfect and beautiful, just like you.'

She stared in silence at the man who had given her the two most precious gifts in the world. 'They are beautiful, aren't they?' she said as she drew in a deep breath. Then, apparently forgetting the others still sharing the tent, she added, 'But we're still never having sex again!'

It was a bumpy ride to the makeshift airstrip where the pilot was waiting. They had travelled slowly in a convoy of four-wheel-drives with the assistance of the other campers.

'I won't get on the plane without Jeremy,' Sophie suddenly announced when the pilot explained that her husband could not fly back. There simply was insufficient room.

'We're at capacity as it is. Your husband will have to drive back to Adelaide.'

'I won't do it,' she said, clinging to her husband's T-shirt. 'I want him with me and our babies, or I won't take the flight.'

Mitchell considered Sophie's request. She had been through so much in the past few hours and her request was not unfair or irrational. The woman was in good health and both babies were healthy and he knew they would more than likely be discharged from the hospital in a week or so. They were both a good weight and had no obvious medical problems.

He crossed to Jade, hopeful that she would agree to take the later flight. Emma was the only choice to travel with Sophie and Jeremy. She was the flight nurse and knew the plane's equipment, and if turbulence occurred it would not be an issue to her. She could also more than adequately meet the three patients' medical needs.

Jade tentatively agreed. 'So we'll fly home later this afternoon, then?'

'Yes,' the pilot explained. 'Head back to the campsite in the four-wheel-drive for a couple of hours until I get back… Or you could hit the road but it would be about a six-hour drive.'

'We'll wait for you to return,' Mitchell said. 'There's been some bad weather and I don't know the condition of the road.'

The pilot nodded and, after loading the passengers, he took off.

Jade watched the plane disappear from sight. She was enormously relived that Sophie and her two beautiful babies were on their way back to the Eastern Memorial with Jeremy and Emma but she felt uneasy that she was on the ground with Mitchell.

One of the drivers from the campsite suggested they all head back to the campsite and have something to eat. Then they could return in two hours for the return flight. It was just before five in the evening and with daylight saving the sun wouldn't set for hours.

Mitchell and Jade agreed.

'I'll call home on the way and let them know you'll be late tonight,' Mitchell said as they climbed into the vehicle for the ten-minute trip back to the campsite. It was quicker going back as they didn't have to take it slowly for Sophie and the babies.

The early vegan dinner was lovely and much needed. Jeremy and Sophie's friends insisted on providing a healthy spread of food as a thank you for all that Jade and Mitchell had done in ensuring Sophie and the babies were fine. Mitchell and Jade didn't realise how hungry they were until they started eating. There was an abundance of everything and it was beautifully prepared and very tasty.

'As I said, Eastern suburbs hippies do the whole Woodstock thing in style,' he whispered in her ear. 'And they take their four-wheel drives to a campsite in the middle of nowhere so they're not exactly roughing it.'

Jade smiled as she took another bite of her salad. 'But maybe next time they shouldn't do it when one of them is heavily pregnant.'

The time was passing quickly and Jade was preparing to head back to the makeshift airstrip when a call came through.

'Dr Forrester, it's Doug from the RDFS base in Adelaide. I'm just calling to inform you that there's been an emergency on a sheep station just north of you and unfortunately the pilot has been redirected there and won't be able to collect you this evening. I can have a plane there in the morning.'

'I guess that will have to be okay. What time do you want us back at the airstrip?'

Jade was busy thanking her hosts for their hospitality.

'Fine,' she heard him say as she headed to the four-wheel-drive. 'We'll be there at nine a.m.'

Jade's jaw dropped. There had to be some mistake.

'Be where at nine in the morning?'

Mitchell drew a breath, well aware that Jade would not like his answer.

'The airstrip.'

'No, we can't be staying here tonight. Why? What happened?'

'An accident at a sheep station is more urgent than us, I'm afraid, so we're here till the morning.'

It was a disaster. Jade was upset and although she knew she had no right to be angry with Mitchell, she still felt that it was his fault in some way. She had never spent a night away from Amber and worried how the little girl would react.

Mitchell saw her stiffen and stare coolly at him. 'I'm not wanting to be here any more than you, believe me. I've done my fair share of camping over the years and I quite like the king-size bed and the air-conditioning I have back in Adelaide. But we need to make the best of it. I'll see if they have a spare tent so we can have one each and we'll get the bedding organised now.'

'But what about Amber? You promised me that I would be back to tuck her into bed.'

Mitchell ran his fingers through his hair. 'I know, and I'm sorry. I didn't plan for this to happen.'

'I never said you did, but I'm worried about Amber.'

'I'll call my mother and you can talk to her and to Amber while I organise our sleeping arrangements.'

Mitchell dialled and handed the telephone to Jade, who was quickly reassured by Maureen that Amber would be fine and that she would sleep in the room with her overnight. Jade felt better. Not great, but better.

Mitchell, however, wasn't feeling so great. He had been told they would have to share the tent that belonged to Jeremy and Sophie. It was a state-of-the-art tent and they did have spare clean sleeping bags and pillows to give them. He decided to deal with that problem later. He worried that if he raised that issue, Jade would start the three-hundred-mile trek home on her own.

'Let's walk around for a while,' Mitchell suggested as his footsteps cracked the fallen pieces of eucalyptus bark lying on the ground. 'Amber is under control back at home and my mother will call if there are any problems. There's nothing to do but make the most of the time here and I promise nothing daring or risky, just a nice bush walk.'

Jade still wasn't happy.

It was her worst nightmare. Stuck so far away from Amber. And with a man she had to admit she was growing fond of, despite her best efforts.

If it weren't for the joy she had seen on Amber's face when she had talked about spending her day with Maureen and Arthur, Jade would have regretted her trip to Adelaide immediately. But she couldn't turn back the clock and neither would she, as Amber, Maureen and Arthur deserved to spend time with each other.

She had to be logical. There was nothing anyone could do to change things. She reminded herself that Amber was settled with Maureen and Arthur and they would no doubt be making a fuss of her so she probably wouldn't be overly anxious. *She* was the anxious one. She told herself it would be just the one night and then she had four days off with Amber. They would celebrate her third birthday with a trip to the zoo. But not the one that Mitchell had suggested with the roaming lions. Jade liked the petting zoo, where they could walk among the goats, and chickens and ducks. She was slowly getting her anxiety under control. Looking for the positives was the best solution, she decided. It wasn't the end of the world. She would spend a few hours seeing some Australian bush wilderness up close before she crawled into her own tent, and then in the morning they would be back in Adelaide.

She just didn't want to get up close to Mitchell. But then she reminded herself that they had a group of campers with them. It wasn't as if anything could or would happen.

Jade looked down at her nursing uniform, now a little the worse for wear and stained with blood. 'I think it might be difficult to hike around in this. I mean, the white duty shoes are about the only bit that works. And you'll look a little silly in your outfit too, a little formal for a bush walk.'

Mitchell looked down at his clothes and realised his long grey slacks and white business shirt and the tie that was hanging loosely from the collar would not be the best outfit.

'Maybe someone can loan us some clothes,' he said, and headed over to the group about to begin their bush yoga class. 'Since we're here overnight, I was just wondering if you might have some clothes we could borrow until tomorrow.'

One of the older ladies in the group slowly undid her very awkward lotus pose with a grimace. 'I have some old things that belonged to my daughter and son-in-law. I meant to drop them at the mission but didn't have time. There's a bag in the car. I'll grab something for both of you,' she said as she stood up. 'And while you're off walking I'll fix up the tent with the new bedding since you'll be staying the night together. We don't have a spare tent.'

Jade felt her stomach fall and heart race. That was not how she had pictured the sleeping arrangements. Sleeping in the same tent with Mitchell had her close to panic.

Lying in the dark hearing him breathing. Knowing he was so close. Knowing he was stirring feelings that she should not be feeling.

Mitchell saw Jade flinch and he knew what he needed to do.

'I'll sleep under the stars and you can have the tent.'

She let a little breath escape with relief and her pulse returned to normal. She couldn't share a tent with Mitchell. It wasn't because she couldn't trust him, it was because she wasn't sure she could trust herself.

'Here you go,' the woman said, and handed Jade some denim shorts and a T-shirt and Mitchell a pair of cargo pants and a tank top. 'They might not be a perfect fit but they'll be better than what you're wearing now for out here in the bush.'

Jade smiled and took the clothes. 'Thanks so much. I'll launder them and drop them off at the mission next week.'

Jade disappeared into the tent and when she emerged, Mitchell's jaw dropped. The tiny denim shorts fitted like a second skin with her long bare legs pouring from them. The tight T-shirt that bared her midriff was also the perfect size, in Mitchell's opinion, but he was sure Jade would not agree. He was certain her *prim and proper* alarm would be ringing.

'I'll check if she has anything else for me to wear. This is obviously for someone a few inches shorter,' she said, tugging at the hem of the top, trying to hide the bare skin.

'I think you look great…in fact, better than great. There's no time to change, the sun will go down and we won't see anything if you try on everything in the mission bag. Let me throw on my hand-me-downs and we can get out of here and take in some sights of the Aussie scrub.'

Jade felt so self-conscious. It had been so long since she had been out in public in revealing clothes and she wanted to pull the denim fabric down to cover her legs as well. But there wasn't any spare fabric and none was about to magically appear. The shorts were so small and the T-shirt was stretched very snugly over her breasts. She was at least grateful she had worn a sports bra and not a lacy number.

Mitchell emerged as if he had chosen the outfit. Jade knew he couldn't have done better with a stylist. The tank top showed off his perfectly sculpted arms and the cargo shorts sat low on his hips, just the way he liked them and the way she had seen him wear them at the beach.

Remembering the fact that Mitchell had already seen her in her bikini, and the others were involved in an Outback yoga class, and the kookaburras definitely wouldn't care about her attire, she decided she had no choice but to let it go.

'Looks like you're about to get your first sighting of marsupials from the land Down Under,' Mitchell said with a smile.

He grabbed some bottled water from the campsite cooler and they headed off through the dry scrub with the leaves and bark snapping under their feet. The air was still dry and warm and Jade could smell the distinctive scent of the eucalyptus leaves. She was thrilled when half an hour into their walk she spied a lizard sunning itself on a hollow tree branch. The brown and black scales blended with the tones of the bush surroundings and it became almost invisible.

'Would poisonous snakes, like rattlesnakes, be around here?' she asked as she surveyed the tufts of dry grass dotted on the red dirt around her.

'There are poisonous snakes, but we don't have rattlesnakes, they're one of your countrymen. I'd say the deadly brown snakes would be the ones to watch out for around here.'

'That's a help.' She laughed as she jumped from one large boulder to another. 'That's the colour of most snakes!'

'Then maybe,' he called to her, 'don't try to pat any of them.'

Mitchell loved seeing that side of Jade. She was carefree and spirited. He wished they could stay here for a week and get to know one another. To see how much more he could uncover about the woman who was now standing atop a two-foot rock and smiling into the setting sun.

She was perfect and he was dangerously close to falling for her.

They were having such a great time that Jade even forgot how inappropriate her outfit was. The Outback and Mitchell were both captivating and distracting. The walk was wonderful with the scent of the warm summer night and the wildlife sounds all around them.

'So how do you like Outback Australia?'

'Well, it's definitely a far cry from LA,' she said as she climbed over some rocks to where he was standing. 'Can you tell me more about where we are?'

'As your personal tour guide—unpaid, I might add—I can.' His mouth curved into a ridiculously handsome smile. 'This is the Flinders Ranges National Park. We're about three hundred miles from Adelaide...' He paused as he realised immediately that it also meant from her niece.

'And Amber,' she added dryly. 'But I'm okay, really.' She decided the rock could be her makeshift seat in the sun as she dropped down onto the hard but warm boulder for a rest while she enjoyed the view. 'I'm sure Maureen and Arthur are spoiling her rotten and, to be honest, I couldn't be happier about it. She needs to know she has family who love her as much as I do.'

Mitchell was surprised. It was a huge step for Jade. He hoped he'd had something to do with her shift in demeanour. She was still far from the wild child that

David had spoken about, but she was even further from the governess in those shorts.

'We all do,' he said, and their eyes met for the longest time.

Jade pointed ahead and purposely broke the spell. 'So what's over there?'

Mitchell didn't want the moment or the feeling to end. For the first time in his life he loved the way he felt about a woman beside him.

Finally, he looked across the landscape and answered. 'Bunyeroo Gorge is about twenty miles from here. It's a great drive with spectacular views and a trip through the gorge itself. The last time I travelled through there, a few years ago, there was a fair amount of water, which added to the driving experience but we won't have time to do it today. Maybe if you want to see more of Australia we could come back.'

Jade was surprised by the invitation. She had not thought past this trip, and definitely not planned that they would spend additional time together, but it made her feel good that he had. She smiled at the thought of exploring the wilderness with Mitchell.

'Some of the rock formations are over six hundred million years old,' Mitchell continued. 'Then there's the Brachina Gorge, which is particularly awesome. It's rugged country but stunning up there.'

'So you've spent a great deal of time travelling around Australia?'

'I backpacked around when I was eighteen. I needed some space of my own and to not be responsible for anyone else so I took off and worked odd jobs to pay my way. I do love Outback Australia.'

'Tell me some of the history,' Jade said, then added, 'Your history, not the gorge's.'

Mitchell took Jade's cue and sat down on a rock not too far from her. 'Not much to say. I travelled a lot after graduating, I told you that in the plane. I worked overseas and I'm back in Adelaide for a while. That's about it.'

'What about your childhood?' she said, lying back a little on her rocky platform above the dirt. 'Did you want to study medicine because of your stepfather? Did he encourage you during your high-school years?'

Mitchell wished that Arthur had been there while he'd been in high school. That would have made his life much easier and particularly his mother's and brother's lives.

'No,' he replied as he waved a horse fly away from his brow. 'Arthur came into my mother's life when I was already in medical school. My father was long gone and she met Arthur when she was working as a dental receptionist. He needed an emergency appointment and she squeezed him in to see the dentist and that was it. Arthur asked her out to dinner after the dentist put in a temporary filling, and they've been together ever since. They say it was love at first sight.'

'What a romantic story,' Jade said as she stretched her legs out in front of her and instinctively curled her toes. 'It sounds like David and Ruby. Theirs was love at first sight too.'

Mitchell said nothing. He couldn't relate to the idea. Falling in love and settling down had always been the furthest thing from his mind. In his mind love didn't last and the collateral damage scared him to the core. But for some strange reason, sitting with Jade, it suddenly didn't seem so unnerving.

'I guess they're the lucky ones,' she said, looking up into the pink and purple striped sky that hung over them like a giant patterned canopy.

'Lucky perhaps the second time around, but not even close with the first,' he said without thinking.

'So her relationship with your father was very unhappy.' She turned to face him, her expression suddenly serious.

'Let's just say he let us all down, shattered the family, but we got through,' Mitchell said, climbing back to his feet. 'Not without some scars, mind you, but it's much too great an evening to waste it talking about my father.'

They walked in silence and enjoyed the sunset. While Jade was curious about Mitchell's father, she didn't bring it up again. He obviously didn't want to discuss it further and that was his prerogative. But it did make her think it might be an underlying reason for his behaviour over the years. His father's actions had definitely impacted on Mitchell.

They were both mindful they needed to be back before it was completely dark. Mitchell had a good sense of direction so he knew they would be safe. Jade realised how she once again she felt safe just being near him. And now knowing a little more about the man, feeling safe with Mitchell wasn't scaring her at all.

CHAPTER EIGHT

'SOMETHING TELLS ME Australian beer is not to Jade's liking,' Mitchell told the other campers. They had returned from their hike and had been invited to join them for a nice cold drink. It was the first time Jade had sampled the amber drink with the white froth and she quickly realised she would never ask for one again.

'It's so…bitter,' she said as her face contorted a little, and she quickly passed the small bottle to Mitchell. Without hesitation, he took a sip.

'It's cold and I'm off duty, so I'm not about to complain.

Suddenly they both realised how comfortable they had become in each other's company. They had a level of familiarity between them that made it natural for him to finish her drink.

The campsite hosts offered Jade a nice chardonnay instead and she quickly found that Australian wine was much more to her liking as they passed the evening with polite conversation. The men then pulled out some cards and suggested poker. Jade noticed Mitchell suddenly shift in his chair. She could see he clearly didn't like the idea, which suited her as she was getting tired. It had been a long day, but she couldn't help but notice there was more to Mitchell's reaction than just tiredness. There was a look of disapproval.

'It's getting late and the plane will be back in the morning, so I think we'll turn in for the night. Thank you all for your hospitality.' Mitchell stood up and with a look that Jade had trouble defining in her own mind he reached his hand down to help her up.

Without thinking, he kept holding Jade's hand long after he needed to and he led her to the other side of the camp and to their tent.

'You don't approve of cards?' she asked as they neared the tent.

'Let's just say I don't think much of anything related to gambling. No one should gamble money, lives...or people's feelings.'

'That sounds like it's coming from a place of experience,' she said softly. She wanted to know more about the man who was making her body and heart come alive.

Mitchell walked farther away from the others, still holding her hand. He sat down on a large fallen eucalyptus branch not too far from their tent and gently pulled her down beside him.

'My biological father gambled with our family and when he lost, we all lost.'

Without thinking, Jade stroked his arm as he looked into the distance and into his past.

'My father lost everything we owned, our home, savings, even my mother's jewellery was pawned before he took off with his mistress when I was only fourteen.'

'Mitchell, I'm so sorry.'

'Hey, we still had each other but in my infinite wisdom as a teenager I decided it was my job to make it up to my mother.'

Jade was confused. 'But it was your father who lost everything and walked out. You had nothing to do with it.'

Mitchell released her hand. His jaw tensed before he spoke. 'I saw him with the other woman. I was catching the tram home from school and I saw him leave the casino, holding hands with a woman I knew worked in his office. It was about six months before he left us. Looking back, I should have said something, maybe prepared my mother. Perhaps we could have secured the house, or at least the money and her jewellery. But I did nothing. I hoped it was a one-night stand, an affair that would blow over. I didn't tell anyone, not even my father.'

'Your mother may not have believed you, Mitchell. She may have thought you were mistaken, and more than likely your father would have lied his way out of it. A man who would do that is not going to admit it.'

'Who knows? But I couldn't change anything so I decided to make it up to my mother and brother and lied about my age, got a false ID and got work in a warehouse. I told my mother that I hated school and got home schooling, which allowed me to work all day and study at night. David was only nine and couldn't help. I just wanted him to stay on track and at school.'

Jade felt tears welling inside. Mitchell had made life choices at such a young age through misguided guilt and enormous reserves of compassion.

'My mother found employment too, but with little or no workplace skills her money was not enough to keep a roof over our heads and pay off the credit-card debt my father had also run up. So we both kept working and I missed out on a huge part of my teenage years. My mother hated that I had to work and she told me she'd work longer hours so I could return to school but we both knew she couldn't work any more hours. There weren't enough in the day for either of us.'

'Your father's selfish behaviour cost you your youth. No wonder you've spent the last few years having fun.'

'It was hardly the coal mines...'

'To a teenage boy, missing out on everything normal and natural and silly in those precious years would be life-changing and devastating,' Jade cut in, aware of her own carefree, rebellious youth.

'Arthur came into my mother's life when I was eighteen. He was a good man and I was very happy to see my mother happy, but I also was over it. I was over being responsible. I took off. It was as though I had handed my mother to Arthur and I was out of there.'

'That's being a little harsh on yourself. I'm sure Maureen was relieved that you no longer had to be the man of the house.'

'I worry that I would have bolted anyway, even if Arthur hadn't shown up. I was burnt out.'

Jade shook her head. 'I'm sure you would have stayed. If you managed to hold it together for three long years, working and studying, you would have seen it through. I'm sure of it.' Her hand reached up and brushed away a stray wattle flower that had landed on his shoulder.

'Nice of you to think so, but I guess I share my father's DNA. Maybe Arthur was a stroke of luck because I was done. That's why I've avoided family. I don't want to let anyone down. I felt trapped. Maybe that's how my father felt when he left.'

'Stop right there,' Jade demanded of the man she had so quickly come to know. 'You were fifteen when you took on the role your father abandoned, you held it down for three years and took care of your mother and brother, and finally, when you mother found love, you left to enjoy your life. How is that anything like a selfish middle-aged man gambling all the family's money, leaving them in debt and shooting through with his mistress? They are poles apart. You showed maturity beyond your years, love and loyalty, while your father's actions were despicable.'

'Maybe that's how you see it but I'm not that chivalrous. And I can't change now,' he admitted.

'I disagree. I think you cut your hair and shaved your beard to meet your niece. You wanted her to like you and not be scared away by the wild bushman. You cared about how she felt. It might seem a little thing but add that to the way you melt around Amber, and it shows the man you are. You have a wonderful heart and you're nothing like your father.'

Mitchell had told himself as he'd sat in the barber's chair the day after he'd arrived in Adelaide that it would be cooler to have shorter hair in the summer, and perhaps this way he wouldn't scare either Jade or Amber away. But he knew inside it was more than that. More than even Jade could see. A part of him wanted to be a little more like David. He wanted to be closer to the father Amber had lost, even if it was only for a few weeks.

But he doubted he could come close to being half the man his brother had been.

'I like to have no roots, I don't want to be in one place or responsible. I don't think that I ever will…'

Jade saw Mitchell in a different light and she cut short his words with a kiss.

He had been running from guilt that he shouldn't have

been carrying and she felt her last walls of resistance fall with his honesty. She now needed to be honest with herself. She wanted Mitchell Forrester.

Looking at Jade, comfortable in her skimpy outfit, enjoying the Outback, Mitchell also saw a different side of her and he couldn't hold back any longer either.

Their bodies only inches apart, her heart was pounding as she felt his breath on her cheek and smelt the scent of his woody cologne. Neither moved. Neither had the strength to walk away. The sincerity and warmth in his words drew her to him and she didn't know what to think any more. She was about to give in to feelings she had never thought she would feel again. The desire that he was stirring she had thought was buried completely under a sea of duty and guilt. With little effort he was resurrecting a side she had thought was lost for ever.

His hands cupped her face before passion took over and there was urgency as his mouth closed on hers. With no need for words, he pulled her close to him and, forgetting their bush surroundings, his hands roamed the curves of her body. Willingly, she pressed her body against the hardness of his and a little groan of pleasure escaped from her lips. She could hardly breathe.

His mouth moved slowly down her neck, trailing kisses across her skin. Her back arched as he gently tilted her head to take his kisses lower.

'Is there room in your tent for both of us?' His voice was low and husky.

She nodded her reply as his tongue teased her skin and he led her by the hand into the darkness of the tent, where he slowly removed every piece of her clothing. And then his own before he was consumed by passion for the woman lying naked on the ground.

* * *

Jade woke in the morning to the sounds of the kooka-burras in the treetops and some rustling in the leaves on the ground outside. She sat upright in surprise.

Then she felt a warm hand pull her back down to the softness of the thick sleeping bag for two.

'It's probably just a possum or koala. Lie back down with me and I'll protect you from ferocious marsupials.'

Her lips formed a soft smile before Mitchell's mouth claimed hers. His kiss held the same level of passion that they had enjoyed during the hours of lovemaking before they'd fallen asleep in each other's arms. It was very clear to Jade that the morning was beginning in the same wonderful way the night had ended. There would be no argument from her.

'Jade,' he began, realising that for the first time in his life he wanted more than a one-night stand. He wanted Jade in his life for ever. 'Last night was wonderful and I hope we can find a way to make this work…'

'Let's take it slow. I don't want you to feel pressured. I wanted you and you wanted me. I am so happy here with you right now. Let's see where this leads.' It was the Jade of old speaking and she was happy to hear that voice from the past. As they lay in each other's arms, they heard voices outside.

'Do possums talk?' she whispered with a smile in her voice.

He put his finger to her lips and softly said. 'Let's pretend we're asleep and they'll go away.'

The male voice drew closer. 'I can't hear you very well, the reception out here is terrible but I'll see if he's awake and get him to call you back.'

Jade drew the covers up as she heard the footsteps next to the zip door of the tent.

'Is anyone awake?' the man's voice called. 'It's quite urgent. There's a call from Adelaide.'

'Just a minute.' Mitchell struggled in a half-kneeling position to pull on his boxers and jeans before he bent down and tenderly kissed Jade again. 'Hold that thought and don't get dressed. I'll be back soon. I'm sure it's nothing. The plane's not due for another hour.'

He unzipped the tent, stepped into the warm morning air and stretched.

'Sorry to wake you but you left your phone out here on the chair and it was vibrating on and off for about ten minutes so I picked it up.'

Mitchell noticed the serious look on Jack's face.

'Who was it?' he asked with concern in his voice.

'Your mother…' he began.

'Is everything all right?' Mitchell could hear the man's voice was sombre. 'Did she say what it was about? Has there been an accident?'

'Not an accident but apparently your niece had a turn of sorts. She's in hospital, something about her kidney failing.'

'I mean, she has another one so I'm sure she'll be all right,' the man said with an inflection that made the statement become closer to a question.

'No, she won't, my niece only has one functioning kidney.'

Mitchell and Jade were driven back to the makeshift airstrip by one of the men from the camp. The plane would arrive half an hour earlier than originally planned to get them to Adelaide. Jade was back in her nursing uniform. Mitchell was had also changed back into his hospital clothes, and they stood under the shade of a giant eucalypt.

'I should never have come.' She scowled at herself. 'I should have insisted that you take another nurse. It just was another bad choice I've made in life. I can't believe what I've done, what *we've* done. I left Amber alone so far away from me. I was stupid and thinking about myself. Last night while we were…' She fumbled over her words, not wanting to admit to what had happened between them. 'Last night Amber needed me and I wasn't there.'

'You mean when I was making love to you.'

'While we were thinking about ourselves and forgetting the real world and our responsibilities,' she corrected him without referring to their lovemaking. 'I let Amber down, and I let Ruby down. It was wrong of me.'

'You didn't let anyone down. We spent the night together, and there was nothing wrong about it.'

'It shouldn't have happened. I came to Adelaide to let Amber meet her grandparents, not to hook up with her uncle.' She bit her lip angrily. Her breathing was laboured as she paced the dusty track and looked up at the sky impatiently.

'Call it whatever you want, but I'm not sorry it happened. I have feelings for you. I'm not sure where it will lead us but last night was not just a hook-up. It wasn't planned and it isn't why Amber is facing health issues right now. The two aren't related any more than the accident three years ago that you still carry around as if you personally caused it to happen.'

Jade shot him a look of contempt. 'You don't know anything about it. I booked the holiday for them. I told them to go and get away to Palm Springs. It's my fault they are both dead and now look what has happened to Amber because of me being away from her. She was probably fretting, I could have stopped it happening…'

'Don't do this,' he said firmly as he walked to where she was still pacing and pulled her to him. 'You couldn't change what happened. You're a nurse and you know that Amber's condition was present at birth and there was every chance this could happen without warning. The nephrologist would have explained that to you before you left Los Angeles to come here. You can't keep Amber in a glass room inside bubble wrap so she can't hurt herself and you can't watch over her twenty-four seven.'

Jade angrily pulled herself free from his embrace. 'I should have refused to come here.'

'You had no choice, you had to travel with me. You were the best nurse for the job. And if it wasn't for you, those two babies might not be alive today.'

'The plane is here,' she said, ignoring his remark about the birth and the positive outcome. It was still not enough to balance out what she had done wrong in her eyes.

There was an uncomfortable silence for the hour's flight. Mitchell did not want to add to Jade's stress or create a scene in front of the pilot. He was grateful that no bad weather was predicted and there was little chance of turbulence as he knew that Jade would never let him help her and he would hate to watch her suffer that anxiety along with the worry of Amber.

With clear skies, Mitchell's focus was on getting back to Adelaide to speak to the nephrologist at the Eastern Memorial. He knew that Adelaide had world-class renal facilities and he would turn every stone and make every call to ensure Amber had the best care.

Amber and Jade now meant so much more to him than he had ever thought possible. Even if Jade didn't want to pursue their relationship, he would always be there for the two of them, however that played out. He was certain it would be from a distance, but that didn't matter. What mattered was Amber.

Jade had caught a cab with Mitchell directly to the hospital as he had insisted on being present to discuss his niece's medical condition with the specialist.

'I can handle it,' she told him tersely when they arrived at the Eastern Memorial.

'I am fully aware that you can and do prefer to do things on your own. But I am here and I want to help if I can. I'm her uncle. I have a right to be there.'

'Just as you have been for the last three years?'

Mitchell ignored the remark. He knew it was deserved and he also knew that Jade was lashing out from fear. He refused to walk away and demanded to meet the renal specialist in his office before they saw Amber.

'What's the prognosis for Amber?' Jade asked as she tried to pretend that Mitchell was not in the room.

'Well, when the kidneys aren't working well, symptoms are varied and may be the same as many other conditions, but when her grandfather, Dr Forrester, Senior, accompanied Amber here last night, he quickly alerted the staff and A and E about her situation. After the initial examination, the senior consultant contacted me immediately and Amber was transferred to the renal unit.

'Amber, I note, has been feeling tired since arriving from the US, but I believe everyone put that down to jet-lag, which is understandable. She has also lost her appetite but, again, in a three-year-old that can be pickiness about food. But it was the swelling in the hands and the associated numbness that concerned Arthur so fortunately he drove her straight in to be seen and we immediately noted high blood pressure. We have tested her urine and it's positive for protein and the bloodwork shows creatinine. As you know, healthy kidneys usually filter both. Her only working kidney is failing. We have her on dialysis now.'

Jade gasped, and Mitchell instinctively moved towards her but she shot him a look that told him everything. His arm dropped away, and Jade moved away to stand alone and receive the remaining news.

'So are we looking at a transplant?' Mitchell asked.

'Yes, I'm checking the donor register now—' the doctor began.

'I want to be tested as soon as possible,' Jade announced. 'Family should prove a better match.'

The doctor nodded his head. 'Sometimes but not always.'

Mitchell found Jade pacing the corridor outside Amber's room a few hours later. She was back to the drab clothing again, which he suspected his mother had brought in for her.

'How's Amber?'

Jade looked in silence at Mitchell. She hated him for the choices she made when she was with him. First the motor bike ride and then…then making love in the tent when she should have been home with Amber. For the way he made her feel and the way she forgot her responsibilities in life. She couldn't be around him. Not now and not in the future. People she loved got hurt when she didn't think things through properly and that could never happen again.

'What is it? Are you still angry for what happened between us? Because I'm not. Together we can help Amber.'

'Amber and I don't need your help. We'll be fine on our own.'

'I know you can cope on your own. You're a strong woman, but you don't have to take on everything alone and think Amber's your sole responsibility. And you have this idea that everything bad that happens is your fault. And that if you behave in a certain way then everyone you love will be safe.'

'What's wrong with that? I love Amber and want what's best, and I know that if I don't watch out for her then something bad can happen. Look where we are today.'

'That has nothing to do with you not looking out for Amber. You left her in the care of my stepfather, who is a retired medic, and he saw the signs and brought her straight to hospital.'

'But I should have been there.'

'Why? What possible difference would it have made?'

'Because it's what Ruby would have wanted and what she would have done. She would have been there. She wouldn't have run off to the bush and slept with a man she barely knew.'

'Stop trying to live your life as if you were Ruby. She was a wonderful woman and my brother loved her. But you're not her. You're an amazing woman in your own right. You have to stop living your life in the shadow of someone else.'

'I'm not now, nor was I ever amazing,' she told him. 'I was shallow and didn't take life seriously. Hardly admirable qualities and definitely not good enough for Amber. She deserves so much more.'

'Having fun and loving life is not shallow in my book,' he told her as he ran his fingers through his hair in frustration. 'What Amber deserves is to know the real Jade. To see that the woman who willingly and selflessly put her life on hold to take care of her niece is not a serious, staid old spinster. Since when does having fun and living life make you less admirable? You didn't hesitate to take on the role of bringing up your niece so I think that makes you extraordinary and you need to stop judging yourself. No one else is. You're the judge and jury.'

'But Ruby was sensible and sweet and a warm and wonderful wife and homebody.'

'And you're not Ruby.'

'She was my sister and I can be like her. I owe it to Amber to be like her mother.' Jade knew even as she said it that it wasn't true. She was nothing like Ruby and that was what troubled her most. How could she be everything Amber needed if she wasn't like her sister?

'Were you ever looking for a man like David?'

'That question is so wrong,' she snapped. 'David was my sister's husband and he's dead. How can you ask that question?'

'It's not wrong. It goes to prove my point. Would you have ever seen a future with a man like my brother before the accident?'

'He was stable and considerate...'

'Was he your type before you became Amber's guardian?'

'No, he was Ruby's type.'

'Then stop trying to be Ruby. You're a wonderful person, Jade, and you should let Amber and the rest of the world see the woman who is hidden inside this shell.'

'But I was irresponsible and crazy and nothing close to what Amber needs.'

'No, you weren't, you aren't and you never could be,' he insisted. 'You stepped up and became the best parent that Amber could hope for while you were still the old Jade. The accident didn't give you time to reinvent yourself. You instantly and without hesitation did what you knew you had to do for your niece. And it was what you wanted to do. Nobody had to force you to do it. Dressing and behaving in a way that mimics your sister isn't going to bring her back or make you a better person.'

'But you didn't know me then, so you can't pass that judgement.'

'I know you now. I know the real you. The woman who was saving those babies then climbing rocks and then sharing a makeshift bed in that tent with me. That was the real Jade.'

'Amber loves me the way I am now...'

'Amber loves the woman who would give her life to make her happy, the woman who has that little girl in her heart so deeply that she is a part of her, but she would love you no matter what the packaging. You don't need to be someone else to have her love.'

'But her respect as she grows older is just as important.'

'Do you honestly think that a teenager is going to be able to relate to her maiden aunt looking and behaving like she stepped from a nineteenth-century novel?'

'I hardly dress or behave like that.'

'Jade,' he said as his fingers softly moved the stray

wisps of hair from her fringe, 'you are behaving exactly like that. I'm not asking you to be someone you're not, I'm asking you to be exactly who you are. A passionate, fun-loving woman who will raise Amber to be the best she can be and allow her to have fun and experience life at the same time. Not someone who will make her fear her own shadow.'

Jade flinched then moved her head away. 'But what if something happens to her along the way? What if she's hurt because I allow her to take a risk, to live life the way I did?'

Mitchell looked into the eyes of the woman he knew had crept into his heart. 'You are here, you are alive, despite the fun you had. Ruby and David were cautious and safe and they are not here to raise Amber. I'm not judging them, they lived life the way they wanted to, but it shows that you can't guarantee a long and healthy future by being pedestrian about life choices. Sure, you don't make ridiculous choices that will put you in harm's way but I don't think surfing or a spin on a motorbike or a Ferris wheel ride are called dangerous by definition.'

'But Amber was admitted to hospital while I was away…with you. Walking in the bush and then sleeping together.'

'Yes, *while* you were away with me, not *because* you were away.'

'That's the same thing,' she argued.

'Not even close,' he returned. 'You did nothing to cause Amber to be admitted. That was decided at conception. Genetics delivered her prognosis and now she needs a donor. It's earlier than her doctor had envisaged, and earlier than any of us imagined. But you can't take any blame for that, neither can I, or anyone in this world.

It's the hand that Amber was dealt and we will do our best to turn it around. And I want us to do it together.'

'But I need to behave in a way that will make Amber proud of me and look at me the way she would have looked at her mother. I took that away from her when I sent her parents on that holiday and now I need to make it up to her. Somehow I need to make sure that Amber doesn't miss out on the upbringing that Ruby and David would have provided if I hadn't...'

'Hadn't what?' he cut in angrily. 'Caused the accident? But you didn't, Jade. You weren't the cause, it was some idiot on the 101 who caused the pile-up and the deaths of innocent people but you were not that person. You generously paid for a holiday for my brother and your sister and they both died. But you were not responsible.'

'You're just trying to make me feel better, but I know the truth and I will spend my life making it up to Amber and trying to be as close as I can to the mother that she will never know.'

'So you'd rather be a poor impersonation of Ruby than a brilliant version of you?'

'It's not like that,' she retorted, tears spilling down her face. 'I know that if I hadn't suggested the trip they would still be here today to raise Amber a certain way, and that's just what I'm doing.'

'That argument doesn't hold any water for me,' he said, holding her shoulders with his hands and forcing her to look into his eyes. 'We don't know what might have happened and whether they would still be alive now or not. Perhaps it was not their destiny to raise Amber. Maybe that was always going to be your role. Perhaps even my role too. Who knows? But we can't change the past. We can just build on what we have. Don't sell Amber short. Let her see the awesome woman you are, not some poor version of her mother.'

'I've managed so far and she seems to be doing okay,' she retorted angrily. 'I know what I'm doing and I'm doing a good job of raising her.'

'You won't be able to keep it up.'

'And you would know that because?'

'Because you will burn out. You are trying to fool the most important person in your world—yourself. You can't keep telling yourself it's okay to live a lie. It will crush you because one day it will become too much. I know that from experience.'

'Loving Amber would never be too much,' she spat angrily. His words cut her like a knife.

'I'm not talking about Amber being too much. I mean the lie you are living, trying to be half the woman you really are. Suppressing how you feel, needing to live up to an unreal image that no one but you wants.'

'One night sharing a bed doesn't mean you know me or have any right to tell me how to live my life. You told me yourself that you've spent the last decade running from anything close to resembling ties or responsibility. Last night was fun but I know in my heart there's the chance you won't stay around. I may be the only one who will be here for Amber after the dust settles. I can't lean on you and have you leave me. And I won't risk putting Amber through that. Just go now before she falls in love with you.'

Mitchell froze. His jaw clenched tightly. He hadn't expected that judgmental side of Jade and it disappointed him. She knew what he had been through as a teenager. The sacrifices he had made to ensure there had been food on the table and the rent had been paid. He didn't want to argue. There was no point. Jade had summed him up before they had met and despite everything they had been through and how close they had grown, deep down her opinion hadn't changed. She didn't trust him.

But he had changed. He had fallen in love with the real Jade Grant. He wanted to see where it could lead. But he couldn't live with a woman not true to herself. Jade had no intention of letting Amber see the real woman who had raised her. She wanted to wrap her in cotton wool and let her grow up scared of her own shadow, and Mitchell didn't want to be part of a charade.

'You're right, Jade. I have no idea.' His chin fell to his chest as he drew a deep and resonating breath and prepared to walk away from the only woman he had ever loved. There was no point arguing. She had won. She could go on living a lie but he wouldn't and couldn't be a part of it.

He leaned in, and she closed her eyes as he tenderly kissed her cheek.

A tear escaped from her eye and ran down her face as she watched the love of her life walk away with nothing she could do to stop him leaving. They were both trapped by their pasts.

CHAPTER NINE

'MY DARLING AMBER, you are loved more than you will ever know and you *will* pull through, and grow into a beautiful young woman who can travel the world, climb the highest mountains and find adventure. We're all praying for you,' Maureen said softly to her granddaughter, who lay sleeping peacefully in the hospital bed with the dialysis machine working through the night by her side.

Jade had fallen asleep in the chair and woke to hear Maureen speaking to her granddaughter. She sat up and rubbed her neck, which was stiff from the awkward position she had been in when she'd dozed off. She was surprised to hear Maureen encouraging Amber to walk in her son's wanderlust footsteps but she didn't bother to set her straight. Amber would not be heading off for any adventures if she had anything to do with it. Especially not with her medical condition.

Jade was angry with herself as much as Mitchell for the hard words they had spoken but they were all true. The night they had shared couldn't change their destiny. Mitchell wanted her to be someone she had left behind. Someone she knew wasn't good for Amber.

'The nephrologist left about two hours ago,' Jade said

while still blinking open her tired eyes. 'And Amber finally fell asleep about an hour ago. We were reading one of the books you brought in.'

It had been three days since Jade had slept in a proper bed. Although everyone had repeatedly suggested she take a break overnight, she'd refused. She didn't want Amber to open her eyes and find an empty room. She had returned home to shower and change while Arthur had kept vigil. And she had eaten a quick meal that Maureen had insisted on before she'd left for the hospital again.

'You really should let me stay tonight. I'm not past it, you know. I only just greeted my sixties.'

Jade knew Maureen's offer was genuine but she didn't want to be away from her niece at this critical time.

'I'm fine, really. You have already done too much for me.'

'Hardly,' Maureen returned, as she sat down next to Jade and patted her hand warmly. 'You're as stubborn as that son of mine. You two are so much alike. So ready to step up and try to fight battles on your own when there are people who want to help'

Jade didn't have the energy to argue. She knew that she and Mitchell were polar opposites except for those few hours they'd shared in the tent that night. A time that Jade would never forget but also a mistake. An error of judgement on her part but one driven by the need to be reminded she was a woman.

Maureen drew in a deep breath but kept her voice to little more than a whisper. 'I remember all those years ago, when his father left us.' Her face suddenly became quite serious as she began talking about the past. 'Mitchell was barely fifteen and David was only nine. Their father had been gambling for a long time without my knowledge. He'd kept up a façade for years and juggled money from one account to the other in an effort to keep up appearances when he lost, and then with a big win we would all head off on another extravagant holiday. One day he'd had enough of living two lives and juggling his gambling debts so he sent an email from his office that the marriage was over, he had someone else and he was moving on.'

Jade knew this was the more detailed version of what Mitchell had already told her. It didn't change anything as she listened to Maureen.

'But for us, there was more bad news to follow. Our family home was heavily mortgaged, the cars were repossessed by the finance company overnight, even my jewellery was missing when I thought at least I could sell that to help us make it through.'

'But wasn't your husband responsible for any of the debt?'

'When everything was sold, we broke even. I didn't have to file for bankruptcy but we walked away with very few possessions and I fell into a sad, dark place. Mitchell thought he had to be the strong one. He took everything on his shoulders as if he had to make it up to me and to his brother.'

Jade knew that was because he had seen his father with the other woman and had never told anyone. Except her.

'When he overheard the landlord demanding the rent I just didn't have one week,' Maureen continued, 'he decided that he would handle it all on his own. David was so young. He had no real concept of the damage that their father had done. He knew that I had to cancel his music lessons for a while, but Mitchell refused to let me cancel the maths tutor for his younger brother. Mitchell knew that David wanted to be a doctor and if his grades fell early in his schooling, Mitchell worried that David might not catch up so he paid the tutor from the money he earned working overtime.'

Suddenly David's admiration for his older brother made sense. It had been a deep-seated and long-held admiration for what Mitchell had done many years before. Mitchell had given so selflessly at an age when most teenagers thought only of themselves.

'Mitchell was gifted academically and didn't need additional tuition and said that he could easily work and fit in his own study load and help David with his other school subjects. He would work long hours in the warehouse after the store had closed, and as much as I argued he refused to cut back until we were on our feet and had money in the bank so the rent was never behind again. We pooled our funds and paid the bills. David worked very hard with his maths so he didn't let his brother down. They had so much love for each other.'

Jade felt a tear run down her face. Mitchell's devotion to his family was deeper than just paying bills. It had been ensuring his brother and mother had been taken care of over his own needs. Such sacrifice at such an early age was very rare. Mitchell had been a very special young man who had taken on an enormous responsibility at a young age.

'You must be proud of your sons.'

'Very, my dear, so very proud,' she said, with tears in her own eyes. 'And then I met Arthur.'

Jade's mouth curved into a smile. 'You deserved to be happy after what you had been through.'

'Thank you. Many women go through much worse than me, but there were a few lean years,' she admitted. 'Arthur asked me to marry him and by that time Mitchell was eighteen. He had finished school with an almost perfect score, and was a little battleworn so he took off on an adventure. I was happy for him but worried that what he had been through would affect him for a very long time. He headed off around Australia and spent many months in the Outback, then trekked through Indonesia and finally to Europe, where he backpacked for two years.'

'And grew a beard to look like a jungle hippy,' Jade added.

'Yes.' Maureen nodded. 'And he kept that beard for years, even when he came back to finish medical school and then specialise in neonatal. Arthur was a surgeon, so he encouraged Mitchell and helped where he could, but Mitchell was fiercely independent. He wanted to do it alone. I'm afraid after his father left he almost became an island. Learnt to depend on himself. I've been so worried that he would end up alone and that would be a waste of such a warm and generous heart.'

Jade nodded in silence. She knew he had a generous heart and she had experienced his warmth first-hand, but it didn't lessen the risk of him leaving without warning. Or change his inability to commit. His father had scarred him but she couldn't take a risk and be hurt. She felt sorry for him but she had to think about Amber.

'His father really destroyed his idea of family and as much as Arthur and I have tried it just hasn't made a difference. I'm not sure what it will take. Or *who* it will take to make him believe in love and family again.'

Maureen leant down and softly kissed her grand-daughter goodnight.

'Are you sure you won't let me stay? Arthur is down speaking with one of his former colleagues and he can run you home for a hot shower and some sleep. I can sit with Amber tonight.'

'Thank you, Maureen, but I'm fine, really. I can get a rollaway if I want but I prefer to sit up, to be honest. I can't really sleep anyway.'

Maureen patted her hand. 'I'll be back first thing in the morning, then. And I'll bring some fresh clothes for you.'

Jade watched her leave the room and then turned to Amber sleeping peacefully and thought back to every-thing that Maureen had told her. It all fell into place. She wondered if Mitchell was trying to finally look past the devastation his father had left behind and reach out to her. *Could she and Amber make him believe in love and family again?* She wasn't sure if he could. And she wasn't prepared to take that risk.

He might wake up one day and just decide it was too hard and leave. She fought sleep, her mind consumed with worry for Amber and the reality that she had pushed Mitchell away, probably for the last time. As her eyes finally closed she knew it was for the best. Mitchell didn't belong in her world any more than she belonged in his.

Morning finally came around and Jade woke just as Amber began to stir. Her eyelashes flickered and she made a little moan but quickly fell back to sleep again.

Jade stretched and then went out to the nurses' station to get some water. It was still early and the night shift nursing staff were finishing up paperwork.

'I can get you a coffee if you'd like,' one of the young nurses offered.

'No need,' came Maureen's voice. 'I picked up a long black for her on the way in.'

Jade saw the slightly tired, smiling face coming towards her with a coffee, something wrapped in a small white paper bag and an armful of clothing.

'And I picked up a ham and cheese croissant to go with it.'

The two women walked back to Amber's room, Jade sipping the hot drink.

'It breaks my heart to see her this way,' Maureen said, her expression turning to one of sadness. 'How long will she need to stay on dialysis?'

'I'm checking today if I'm a tissue match and can be Amber's donor. We're both blood type O so we're compatible on the first level so now we just need to undergo the HLA or tissue typing.' Jade put the fresh clothes on the seat beside her and began to unwrap the croissant.

'What does that mean?'

'Well, there are six antigens that have been shown to be the most important in organ transplantation. Of these six antigens, a child inherits three from each parent. It's extremely rare outside identical twins for a six-antigen match between two people, but I hope that we may have more than one matching since I'm a blood relative. Kidneys can be transplanted between two people with no matching antigens without a rejection episode but if by chance we had the six matching antigens then it would mean less anti-rejection drugs for Amber.'

'That's a little confusing but I guess it means if you match then you will have the surgery and Amber will receive your kidney?'

'There's another test called a cross-match test and it's a very important part of the living donor work-up and it's repeated again just before the transplant surgery. Some of my blood and some of Amber's blood will be mixed in the lab. If Amber's cells attack and kill the donor cells, the cross-match is considered positive. This means Amber has antibodies "against" my cells, but if they don't then the cross-match is negative and we're considered compatible.'

'I think you are very brave to donate a kidney to Amber and she's very lucky to have such a wonderful, generous aunt.'

Jade shook her head dismissively. 'No, I'm the lucky one.'

The nephrologist arrived about twenty minutes later. Jade had finished her much-needed breakfast and changed into another skirt and blouse in the bathroom while Maureen watched Amber.

Amber had woken and was able to be taken off the dialysis machine. She was uncomfortable and unsettled but happy that both Jade and Maureen were there.

'I just need you to sign the final consent forms for Amber's surgery.'

Jade was confused and she didn't try to mask it from the doctor. 'But I haven't undergone the tissue matching yet. My appointment is later today.'

'We have a match already. The patient is being prepped and that's why Amber was fasting overnight.'

Jade and Maureen both looked up to notice the sign by her bed. The nurse had come in while Jade had been asleep and put it up so the morning shift would not provide breakfast to the little girl.

'I don't understand. I thought family provided the best possible match.

The doctor approached Jade. 'As I said a few days ago, the likelihood of a perfect match other than an identical twin is about one in ten thousand. Well, it looks like we found our one in ten thousand so there is no need for you to be tested. We already have a perfect match for Amber. He's being wheeled into Theatre as we speak.'

'How did you find the match? Was the person on file already?'

'No.' The doctor hesitated. 'Mitchell underwent the tests two days ago.'

Jade rushed into the ward to find Mitchell being prepped.

'Why are you doing this?' she asked. 'I could have been a match and you wouldn't have to go through this.'

'You've done enough for Amber already. Now it's my turn.'

'This is ridiculous, Mitchell. I never expected you to be the donor. Regardless of the HLA results, if my cross-match is compatible then we can have the operation in the next few days.'

'I'm sure you could, but I'm compatible. End of story.'

Jade closed her eyes in disbelief and frustration. She didn't need Mitchell to offer a kidney from a misguided sense of duty. He was free to leave. Jade knew she would never forget what they had shared but she would survive a broken heart. She didn't want to trap Mitchell into staying. Or into taking on more than he wanted to or more than he could promise to do willingly.

'Mitchell, I finally know you well enough to see that you are trying to fulfil some role you think you should, but you don't. I'm a big girl and I can handle it. I've taken care of Amber since she was born. I can keep doing it.'

'But what if I don't want you to handle it on your own? What if I want to be part of the solution? Don't I get a say in it?'

Her voice was shaky. Amber was deteriorating by the day. They needed to find a donor but this could drastically change Mitchell's life. It was not a small ask to donate a perfectly healthy functioning kidney. He loved to lead the life of a nomad. This might change things. She loved him too much to see him like a bird in a cage.

'Let me get tested and if I'm a fail then maybe you can think about it, but don't rush in to this surgery,' she pleaded.

'You don't get it, do you? I'm doing this because I want Amber to have a long and happy life. I don't want her tied to a dialysis machine. I want her to go sky-diving, and windsurfing and anything else she wants to do. Just like you did and just like I did.'

'But she might not want to do those things.'

'That's true, but if I can give her my kidney I'm giving her the option to have fun and be a little wild, like her aunty was when she was young…and still can be, if she wants to.'

'But I'm not young any more. I have responsibilities and I won't let Amber down.'

'You could never let anyone down. It's not who you are. You would step up to the plate no matter where you were or what you were doing. Even a blind man could see your devotion to Amber but you shouldn't let it control and drive fear into every aspect of your own life. I've seen fun Jade, and I think it's a waste to put her away for even one moment longer.'

'But I don't want to be like that any more. Look what happened when I was irresponsible. Amber ended up in hospital.'

'Her genetic condition sent her to hospital. The fact we spent one amazing night together had no impact on Amber's health. If you had been tucked up in the bed next to hers, she would still have needed hospitalisation, and you know that's a fact. But it's a fact you don't want to face. Maybe because you think if you wrap her up in cotton wool and keep yourself near her, and behave more like her great-grandmother then nothing bad can befall her. It can, Jade. Good and bad things can happen to those we love and trying to control their lives won't change what is destined to happen by way of their genetic make-up.'

'Why are you trying so hard to make me see things your way?' she pleaded as she dropped her shaking head into her hands. 'And why do you want to put yourself through all this? It may change your life and not for the better.'

'Because I believe in my heart that you won't be happy without me and I won't be happy without the real you. Not some cardboard cut-out of another woman. And because Amber deserves to have two loving parents.'

'What do you mean, two loving parents?'

'The two of us. I'm not going anywhere, Jade.'

'But you hate feeling trapped, you said it.'

'That's true, and it still stands. I would never want to be trapped, but being with you and Amber is the opposite. It's the only place in the world I want to be. It's so far from being trapped…it's being wanted, and needed and loved, and it's a place I never want to leave. It's the true meaning of family. If you'll have me, I'll stay for ever.'

'For ever…in one place…with us?'

'I would take more than for ever if I could. I love you, Jade, and I'm here to stay, albeit down one kidney in a few hours. But if you don't want me minus a part, I'd understand.'

Jade didn't want to fight her feelings any more. She leaned down to the man being wheeled into Theatre and kissed him with all her heart.

'You're perfect any way you come.'

EPILOGUE

THE DATE MITCHELL and Amber chose to become husband and wife was one year to the day of the surgery to give Amber a healthy, happy life. With each passing minute Mitchell and Jade knew their love was growing stronger and would last for ever.

Australian immigration had granted extensions to Jade's and Amber's visas on compassionate grounds. Amber had needed time to heal after the surgery and after six months she and Jade had returned to Los Angeles briefly to say goodbye to the kind neighbours who had been like family to them. While it had been sad for everyone, it had been a new beginning for Jade and Amber, and the lovely older couple were happy that the little girl would be with her real grandparents.

Jade had packed up the house and put it up for lease. It was Amber's home and for that reason Jade had chosen not to sell it. She wanted it to be there in case, as an adult, Amber wanted to spend some time in the city where she'd been born. A lovely family who had relocated from Sacramento, with two small girls and a golden Labrador, had moved in, and Jade felt sure her neighbours would shower the little girls with attention, just as they had Amber since she was born.

Mitchell had proposed twice. Once to Jade with a solitaire diamond ring as they rode the Ferris wheel at Glenelg and then a week later he proposed that he and Jade adopt Amber. He didn't want them to be just her legal guardians as he wanted all their children in the future to have the same mother and father.

Amber was four and although she didn't really understand what adoption meant, she loved the idea of having a mummy and daddy like the other children at pre-school. Jade was so deliriously happy she thought she would burst. And so the very special wedding date was set and the adoption papers were filed. And Maureen stepped into one of her happiest roles of her life... and one she had never thought would be hers...the role of wedding planner.

The wedding guests chatted happily under the clear azure sky. They sat on white deck chairs in rows on the lawn, each chair decorated with a huge organza bow. The day was perfect, the guests had all arrived and the celebrant and solo violinist were both eagerly watching for movement from the small white marquee that held the bridal party.

Maureen, beautifully designer dressed and beaming, emerged from the marquee in a mint-coloured silk suit and signalled with a subtle wave of her lace handkerchief.

The solo violinist sat upright, adjusted his jacket and then began "Wedding March" by Felix Mendelssohn. All heads turned back to see Amber hug her grandmother before she took her first tentative step. She looked like a tiny angel in her ankle-length pastel pink silk dress. A circle of fresh rosebuds and gypsophila sat atop her blonde curls and a smile dressed her cherub-like face as she walked down the white carpet aisle, scattering rose petals with each tiny step.

Mitchell's mouth curved into an equally big smile as he caught sight of her. She was walking towards the jasmine-covered arbour where he stood with his grooms-men. His legs, hidden by the black designer suit, were shaking a little as the much-anticipated moment of his bride's entrance drew closer. Amber tried to stay in time to the strains of the violin but she gave up and happily skipped the last few feet.

'You look so pretty,' Mitchell told her as he bent down and kissed her forehead then took her tiny hand in his.

'You thould thee Mummy.' She beamed. 'She lookth like a printheth.'

'I bet she does.'

Alli and Laura appeared from the marquee in their floor-length pale pink silk bridesmaid's gowns and slowly made their way to the arbour. The shoestring straps of their dresses were embellished with tiny crys-tals, their hair was softly curled and falling around their shoulders, and they each held posies of roses and gyp-sophila. All eyes were on them until moments later Ar-thur escorted Jade onto the white carpet walkway.

Mitchell felt his heart stop for a moment. His wife-to-be was breathtakingly beautiful. Her cream silk dress clung to her body like a second skin. It was nothing close to a maiden aunt's attire. The halter neckline was trimmed in crystals and her shaking hands held a posy of pink rosebuds. A delicate short veil skimmed her bare shoulders but allowed Mitchell and the wedding guests to see her beautiful smiling face.

With short steps, she walked towards the man who

had shown her that it was okay to be herself. The man who would not let her live a life carrying guilt or regret. The man who had captured her heart and given her love in return was waiting for her and holding the hand of the most precious little flower girl. His daughter.

Each step brought her closer to the most important people in her universe.

They were all she would ever need.

Arthur finally released Jade's hand to the security of Mitchell's.

'You look beautiful,' Mitchell told her as he held her hand tightly.

Jade smiled at her soon-to-be husband. With one hand holding Amber and the other firmly clasping Jade's, the three of them stood before the celebrant.

'We do,' Amber suddenly called aloud.

The guests all laughed at the little girl's impromptu announcement, and Mitchell turned to face Jade with an overwhelming feeling of desire and love surging through his body.

'I guess if Amber can't wait…neither can I.'

Mitchell gently released Amber's hand. Throwing tradition to the wind, he lifted Jade's veil, swept her into his arms and just before his mouth met hers he whispered, 'I will love you for ever, Mrs Forrester.'

* * * * *

MILLS & BOON®

It's Got to be Perfect

* cover in development

When Ellie Rigby throws her three-carat engagement ring into the gutter, she is certain of only one thing. She has yet to know true love!

Fed up with disastrous internet dates and conflicting advice from her friends, Ellie decides to take matters into her own hands. Starting a dating agency, Ellie becomes an expert in love. Well, that is until a match with one of her clients, charming, infuriating Nick, has her questioning everything she's ever thought about love…

Order yours today at
www.millsandboon.co.uk

MILLS & BOON®

THE ULTIMATE IN ROMANTIC MEDICAL DRAMA